WOLF

The North-South conflict was at its height. With the face of Red Legs, who had killed his parents, branded into his memory, Wolf Strange took to the vengeance trail and became a Missouri Raider. Killing was the order of the day. The Civil War finally ended, but there would be no amnesty for Wolf and his men. There was no option but to flee the territory. But a thousand miles from Missouri, Wolf was to face death again . . .

Books by Elliot Long
in the Linford Western Library:

WASSALA VALLEY SHOOTOUT
DEATH ON HIGH MESA
TRAIL TO NEMESIS
A KILLING AT TONTO SPRINGS
SHOWDOWN AT CRAZY MAN CREEK
MANKILLER
BUSHWHACK AT WOLF VALLEY
RETRIBUTION DAY
GUNTALK AT CATALEE

ELLIOT LONG

WOLF

Complete and Unabridged

LINFORD
Leicester

First published in Great Britain in 2000 by
Robert Hale Limited
London

First Linford Edition
published 2001
by arrangement with
Robert Hale Limited
London

British Library CIP Data

Long, Elliot
    Wolf.—Large print ed.—
    Linford western library
    1. Western stories
    2. Large type books
    I. Title
    823.9′14 [F]

    ISBN 0–7089–9751–1

Published by
F. A. Thorpe (Publishing)
Anstey, Leicestershire

Set by Words & Graphics Ltd.
Anstey, Leicestershire
Printed and bound in Great Britain by
T. J. International Ltd., Padstow, Cornwall

1

Missouri — Kansas border, November 1863

Brutally, Hetch Kinder pulled his sweating, muddy mount to a slithering halt on the edge of the trees. A slow smile broke on his bearded face. Peering from under his sodden hat, his blood-hungry excitement shone in his cruel features.

'I tell you, boys,' he said, 'thet sonofabitch Henry Strange is about to git his. I've waited ten years fer this. Was a time he called me a damned liar, then hid behind his Quaker piety.'

'An' was you a liar?' Sitting beside him, Mitch Layton stared at him. He took little trouble to hide his contempt.

Kinder glared, meanly. 'Thet's beside the damned point.'

'An' you've held it in your craw, all

1

this time?' Layton shook his head, hitched uneasily in the saddle atop his equally hard-ridden roan gelding. His grey gaze was searching.

Kinder met it with a bone-hard, ice-blue stare. 'You bet yer damned life I have, mister.'

To emphasize his grim delight, Kinder spat brown juice on to the colourful, damp leaves covering the ground and gave out with his harsh, rasping laugh. He fumbled under his rain-shiny yellow slicker, pulled his cap-and-ball Colt Army. Now he stared out from the screen of trees across the nearby overflowing creek. The Strange homestead looked friendly, inviting, nestled at the foot of the wooded east side of the valley, blue smoke rising gently from the stone stack into the cool, autumnal air.

All around everything was dripping and grey after the incessant rain he and his men had put up with these past four days. But he didn't even consider the other discomforts they had undergone — the long, nerve-stretching rides raiding through hostile country; the continuous proximity of danger and the constant possibility of sudden death that stalked the trail with them. He and the men with him had long since grown used to that. And now — he stared covetously at the farm — by some heaven-sent twist of fate, a long-held grudge was about to be settled. He'd bet money that bastard Strange didn't even remember the event that had caused Hetch Kinder so much anger and pent up humiliation these past years.

As if sensing Kinder's vicious glee, Mitch Layton moved uneasily by his side allowing his pale, wasted face to express the concern he was feeling. 'Personal prejudice aside, Kinder, I wanna git this straight — has Strange come straight out an' said he's agin Kansas an' the Union?'

Kinder swivelled his cold, blue stare away from the house. 'How in the hell should I know? Damn it, you gonna start bitchin' agin, Layton?' He glared. 'We git our orders. You were there when Charlie Jennison told us Senator Lane was sick to death o' these Beely Creek trash pretending to be sittin' on the fence while givin' comfort to every low-down Missouri raider hidin' out around here.' Kinder cut damp air with a big, bony hand. 'It's time fer examples to be made. We need this area cleared so there's not an ounce of cover or respite left fer those God damned bastards playin' hell with our state. Jest what t' hell is it with you, mister?'

Layton twisted his lean features into doubt. 'Jest thet I wus neighbours with the Strange folk. One time my family lived on a homestead not four miles down the crick from here. An' another thing, I ain't never bin comfortable bein' a Jayhawker, leave alone bein' one o' these Red Legs. When this here war took off, I allus had my sights set on enrollin' with the regular army, not havin' to run around with *irregulars*.'

Kinder's mud-spattered, auburn-bearded visage turned nasty. His anger glowered out of his red-veined, combat-strained eyes. 'You do what you're damn-well told, y'hear? Yuh git local knowledge, an' thet's what you're here fer. Damn it, git it through yer skull, Layton' — Kinder patted the red sheepskin wrappings on his legs — 'this is who you are right now, a damned Red Leg, an' you'd better settle fer it. These here fleeces is our insignia, just like a soldier boy wears a uniform.' He waved his Colt at the homestead. 'Thet there heap of piety is about to git what he deserves, an' thet's final.'

Layton jutted his square chin. 'Jest thet Henry Strange ain't come down on any side, far as I know. Jest wants to be left alone. Allus been thet way with him. He'd help a Union man jest as quick as a Reb.'

Kinder scowled. 'An' yuh believe thet?' Harsh doubt smeared his heavy features. 'Well, let me tell you, mister, you'd best git your haid clear on this.

Charlie Jennison wants a lesson taught around here an' thet's how it's gonna be. You hear me?' Kinder weighted the cap-and-ball Colt Army in his hand. He made no effort to disguise his impatience, or his intentions. 'Now, mister,' he said, 'you still about to argue? You've got ten seconds to decide.'

Layton stared at the Colt pointed at him, then looked up to see the clear, murderous intent in Kinder's bleak eyes. Then he gazed at the other grim-faced riders around him, obviously on Kinder's side. Kelsy Jaul, Zack Boles, Bone Head Jimmy Gains and Willy Rawlinson. It wasn't supposed to be like this, Layton thought. He joined the Kansas Jayhawkers in the late 1850s, thinking he was going to nobly serve the cause for the emancipation of the black man. Instead, he found he had become a member of a bunch of men who were slowly degenerating into a band of cut-throats, no better than those on the other side of the fence — William Clark Quantrill's renegades and now Bloody Bill Anderson's mob, after his break with Quantrill. Missouri-based raiders abounded. And — he glanced across the river — he couldn't be bone-hard certain Strange *wasn't* involved with the Confederate irregulars.

Kinder's Colt clicked menacingly, near his ear. 'You in, or out? Time's awastin'.'

Layton met Kinder's uncompromising stare. For one burning instant he had a desire to tell him to go to hell, but duty, as well as self-preservation, got in the way . . . again. One time, back on the trail a way, he thought he'd be able to talk Kinder out of touching the Strange place, but he hadn't known then of Kinder's hate for the Quaker.

He swallowed on a dry throat, stared at the unwavering Colt. His words, as he forced them out, were like bitter gall. 'When you put it thet way . . . in.'

Kinder's hard features lit up with a grin of triumph. 'Thet's more like it.'

His heart thumping, hating his tame

submission and turning away from the bloodthirsty, gloating Kinder, Layton stared at the homestead across the creek. He saw Henry Strange coming out of the barn, carrying long pieces of split willow in the crook of one arm. As the homesteader passed the plough oxen loitering in the yard he whacked them, sending them towards the grass near the trees at the foot of the steep, wooded hillside. Then Layton noticed something he never expected to see: Henry Strange carrying a rifle. Had the sparse-talking Quaker finally decided to take up arms? Layton found that possibility helped to lighten his fretting conscience. Leastways now, it looked as though Strange was prepared to defend himself.

As he watched Strange draw closer to the house, Heidi, his wife, came out and joined him. Layton saw her flaxen tresses were as he always remembered them, done up in plaits and fastened against her small round head. He knew of her German ancestry, but also knew she was second generation American. Nevertheless, her Teutonic roots were still strong enough to require her only child to be named Wolfgang.

Remembering the boy prompted Layton to look alertly about him. Wolf was nowhere to be seen. For moments, hope welled up in him. Maybe Henry Strange had got his son to a safer place and out of this. He earnestly hoped that was the case.

But now desperate regret jarred through Layton. The times he'd eaten at the Strange table. He was only a few years younger than Henry Strange. Their families had come into the valley from Indiana about the same time. They farmed the same land before he and his kin had decided to move into Kansas and had left the valley. Now he fretted about why Strange hadn't gotten out before they arrived. He surely must have been warned they were on the rampage and heading this way.

Because of that, Layton now felt resentful anger. But, he knew his wrath shouldn't be directed against Strange. It should be aimed more at that damned renagade William Clarke Quantrill and his recent, savage raiding into Kansas. The final straw had been Quantrill's brutal sacking of Lawrence, not three months ago, and the slaughter there of 142 people. Senator Lane lived in Lawrence and, it was rumoured, had been warned of the imminence of the attack and had escaped death by ignominiously fleeing to hide in a nearby cornfield. Opinion was, Quantrill's purpose behind the raid was to find the Kansas senator and kill him. But all Quantrill succeeded in doing was to enrage Lane and give him the perfect excuse — not that he ever needed one — to viciously retaliate against Missouri, which frequently harboured Quantrill and his gang when he wasn't on his bloody raiding. And, to allow him to do that, the senator swiftly invoked Order 11.

With the ink hardly dry on the paper, Lane gave General Thomas Ewing firm orders to implement the edict with all haste. The mandate called for the immediate depopulation of the Kansas-Missouri border by any means deemed necessary.

Startling Layton, Kinder bawled, his voice high with excitement while waving his Colt above his head, 'OK, boys. Let's git it done!'

As he roared Kinder sent his big mud-spattered chestnut gelding out of the dripping trees and across the meadowland towards the creek, sodden turf flying up from the horse's hooves.

Galvanized by his abrupt move, Layton, his pulses thumping up to racing speed, followed him, straight into the swollen, muddy creek. As he hit the icy water the impact of it shocked the breath out of him. Flanking him each side and with wild Red Leg whoops Kelsy Jaul, Zack Boles, Bone Head Jimmy Gains and Willy Rawlinson also committed themselves to the charge.

Now the valley became a bedlam of hoarse yells. Above their harsh shrieking

Layton heard Heidi Strange scream. Then he saw and heard Henry Strange shouting to her as he waved her towards the house. His instructions given, the Quaker turned and raised his long, outdated Hawken rifle and pointed it straight at their charging bodies.

Layton ducked instinctively as the flat crack of Strange's gun rent what peace was left in these river bottoms. Its report sent echoes rebounding up the long, mist-filled valley. Raucously cawing rooks sprang out of their roosts in the trees, to wing like burnt-paper shapes across the lowering, leaden sky.

Mingled with the recurring noise, to his left, Layton heard Willy Rawlinson's harsh cry. He turned to see his comrade falling back off his horse, obviously hit with Strange's bullet. Rawlinson's lifeless form splashed into the water and immediately began floating down the river. Whistling its fright, Rawlinson's startled horse set off at a mad run out of the river and galloped along the bank and back into the trees, stirrups flapping wildly about its flanks and barrel.

As Rawlinson's body sank from sight, Layton heard howls of outrage coming from the men around him. A certain amazement filled Layton to hear them. What, in God's name, sort of reception did the crazy bastards expect when they began this charge across the river? Hominy grits and chicory-loaded coffee? For it was a mortal fact that a visit from the Grim Reaper amongst them was long overdue. In 300 miles of hard riding and creating bloody mayhem, miraculously, Rawlinson was their first casualty. Nevertheless, Layton regretted it had to be Rawlinson. He had been a lively man, good to have about camp. He also knocked out a fair tune on his concertina. For sure, it should have been Kinder.

In reply the boys started to set up a vicious barrage. Acrid gunsmoke soon began stinging Layton's nostrils. Its biting tang once more set in motion the familiar headiness of battle madness.

His reservation about what was happening here now swiftly buried itself in the urgent drive for blood and to avenge Rawlinson's death.

He found himself yelling with the rest, his frenzy building up in him. He knew if he kept telling himself this was right, he would sleep better. Damn it, he had ridden into Lawrence the day after its sacking. Though used to bloody death, he had almost thrown up his breakfast at the sights he saw. Unarmed civilians, shot to hell; grieving women made demented by being forced to watch the slaughter of their loved ones. Damn Quantrill. Damn the men that sheltered him.

As he drew closer, he swept the homestead's confines with his grey, maddened stare. He saw Heidi Strange, obeying her husband, running for the homestead; saw her scuttle in through the door and slam it to. All the time she ran she shrieked her fear.

Now Layton swung his gaze to Henry Strange. The Quaker was trying to reload his ancient long rifle with his powder horn, while all around him bullets savaged splinters out of the wattle fence he was backed against.

There seemed to be a massive aura of calm about Strange and a determination to make a fight of it. While he worked at the loading of his Hawken, the Quaker cast undeterred glances at their oncoming charge. Layton found admiration welling up for his one time neighbour's show of defiant courage.

Then a bullet found Strange and Layton saw shock distort the Quaker's cool look. The lead's impact knocked Strange back against the wattle. Immediately blood began running from his chest. The next bullet to hit drove him half through the wattle fence. That one caused him to cry out harshly, drop his rifle and move his hands to explore his wounds. They soon became bloody. Finally, like a limp rag doll, Strange slithered down what was left of the wattle and ended up slumped against its standing remains, his grey eyes staring out from his gaunt face at their headlong ride.

Still staring at the Quaker, while driving his horse up the bank and out of the flooded creek, Layton heard the sound of glass breaking. It came from the homestead. There, chasing out the shattered glass, he saw a twin-barrelled shot-gun thrust ominous fingers through one of the narrow windows. Immediately, the gun belched smoke and flame, but the range made the shots ineffectual. Meantime, fifty yards in front of him, he saw Hetch Kinder reach Henry Strange and dismount by him.

Kinder, towering over the home-steader, kicked Strange's dropped rifle out of reach of the settler's frantically clawing fingers whilst bellowing to Kelsy Jaul, who was drawing rein by him, 'Git over there an' burn thet crazy damned woman outa there before she does some real damage.'

Jaul's eyes rounded. He looked

stupid, as always. 'What with?' he yelled.

'God damn, think o' somethin', will ya?' roared Kinder while wrathfully he bent to deal with Henry Strange, who was now trying to get up and fight, despite his wounds.

The shot-gun roared from the cabin again. This time it brought a howl of pain from Bone Head Jimmy Gains who was riding past the window, heading towards the barn. A glance told Layton Gains's right leg and his horse's right flank had been mashed by the birdshot.

Gains's horse reared, neighing shrilly, kicking air, sending Bone Head's bulky frame toppling from the saddle. He bounced as he hit the ground. Right off, while looking fearfully over his shoulder, he set to cursing as he began to scramble crab-like for the shelter of the wattle fence, dragging his Spencer carbine with him. Once in cover he opened up on the house while continuing to stream out oaths at the building.

17

Layton saw the heavy lead from the gun begin splintering the weathered clapboard timbers.

Now Layton glared at Kelsy Jaul as he rode in close to him. Jaul was clearly racked with indecision, floundering for ideas as to what to do about Kinder's order to fire the house. As he came alongside him Layton bawled, 'We'll look for oil lamps in the barn.'

Instantly, Jaul's sallow face expressed relief. 'Hell, thet's it,' he said.

He grinned from ear to ear. Layton knew the dumb bastard had grown to love this kind of savage raiding and killing, so long as he didn't have to think about it overmuch. He'd known Jaul a fortnight; hadn't liked what he'd found. The murderous little shit would smile as he killed. If somebody ordered him to do something, no matter how heinous, he'd do it; would never question it. Yesterday, Layton saw him cripple Jack Lawson, who had the homestead thirty miles up the creek, with leg shots, then bend to cut his throat just enough to watch him die slowly and painfully as the blood drained out of him.

Inside the barn, Layton's excited gaze found two lamps and a barrel with COAL OIL painted on it. Jaul was already reaching for the lamps. He picked them up and shook them, grunting his satisfaction when he heard liquid swilling in them.

Gaining his side, Layton said, 'Set them down.' While he spoke he fumbled for sulphur matches in pockets under his shiny yellow slicker. Finding them he kindled the lamps.

While he fumbled, Jaul said excitedly, 'I'll git the barrel. We'll dowse the house. We'll soon have thet crazy bitch cookin' like a spit-roast hog.' His crazy laugh reached above the noises outside.

But Layton found the ghastly statement jarred him. Heidi Strange ... roasting like a hog? That kind, gentle woman he'd known for years before this damned bitch of a war? Once more it set him questioning the right of this. He said urgently, 'Maybe we should bide our time. Maybe we can coax her to come out. I ain't into killin' women, damn it. Never have been.'

Jaul's delight fell off him like a shorn cloak. His black stare became cold. 'You serious? Damn it, ain't she just stitched up Bone Head?' He scowled. 'You ain't thinkin' good, mister.' His stare drilled deeper. 'The bitch's out to kill us, y'hear? She ain't goin' to give up to anybody, no matter what. By God, you'd better also know — next time you show white Kinder'll pull thet damned trigger.'

Though stung by that, Layton glared, but he knew all of it to be true. Kinder would shoot him soon as look at him and women like Heidi Strange could be just as courageous and deadly in their dying as their men. But, once more, the words that spilled out of him were like bitter dregs. 'You're right, I guess. Let's git to it.' Blocking everything else out of his mind he picked up the lamps and moved to the door of the barn. Jaul grunted as he took the weight of the barrel in his arms. He commenced to stagger along beside him.

Stepping out of the gloom of the barn and into the drizzle, the first thing Layton saw was Kinder. He now had a rope around Henry Strange and was remounting his excited horse, in preparation to drag the Quaker. And, as if Heidi Strange was seeing what was happening to her husband, her shotgun roared defiantly from the cabin once more, clearly aimed at Kinder. But the charges went wide, spattering with a rattle into the wattle fence. Kinder turned wrathfully and sent off three shots at her before turning to them and roaring, 'Git it done, damn you!'

Now Strange's woman began shouting wildly in German. And, Layton realized, as they approached, using as shelter the gable of the house, for some bizarre reason, the woman's incessant cursing was now incensing him.

He began bawling angrily at her, 'Shut yer mouth you fool woman!

You've brought this on yerself!' And, craziest of all, the outburst seemed to suddenly cleanse him of all responsibility. The woman was asking for it, like Jaul said. She should have kept out of it, like Cissy Lawson had done yesterday. He had managed to talk Kinder out of harming her. He could have done so here if Strange's woman had stayed still and shut up.

He reached the shelter of south side of the house. Jaul yelled in his ear, 'I'll wash the gable end with this oil, then toss the rest inside through thet window.'

Meantime, Hetch Kinder began whooping, causing Layton to turn. He saw Kinder was now towing Henry Strange up and down the front of the house on the end of his rope, as if taunting the woman. And Strange was clearly still alive, for he was feebly yelling out with pain. Then, abruptly, Kinder began his awful laughing. He veered off towards the strip of rocky ground at the base of the hillside at the back of the homestead. As they disappeared into it, Heidi Strange began keening and Layton recognized a finally demented, stricken woman. He tried to shut the noise out and turned to his work.

Jaul giggled hysterically beside him. 'Jest lissen to thet crazy bitch!' He began smashing out the nearest gable window. Layton saw mad light was burning in Jaul's eyes. When Jaul had done, he turned, his bucked, tobacco-stained teeth exposed by his mad grin. 'Throw the damned lamps in.'

Layton found himself operating as if he was a mechanical doll — abstract-edly, without any need for thought. That had always been his trouble . . . thought. If he could be just be a mindless killer like Kinder or Jaul, God damn it he could live with this.

He sent the lighted lamps flying through the window to crash against the opposite wall of the room. Their glass funnels splintered and fuel spilled, igniting immediately. Yellow flames began to snake across the tinder-dry, rough-hewn floor, chasing the flowing fuel like the flicking tongue of a snake towards the big, comfortable bed and the dressing-table covered with trivia a woman would use to pretty herself.

Beside him, Jaul sloshed fuel from the barrel on to the side of the homestead wall, then, still grinning, he said, 'We'll have ourselves a real blaze here. What yar say we git some hay frum the barn, help it along?'

Fully carried along by the madness now, Layton found himself back in the barn gathering armfuls of hay. Returning to the house with Jaul giggling by his side, he pushed the hay against the fuel-soaked wall and kindled it.

He could hear Heidi Strange's keening had reduced to a despairing moaning. Another thing: there was no firing coming from her. Had she run out of loads? Or, like a terrified, resigned animal was she waiting for her death? Maybe he could break in, drag her out, save her. But no, that wouldn't do. She had picked up a gun. Jaul, or Kinder, or Bone Head, or Zack Boles would still kill her just the same; shoot her down like a dog as soon as he brought her through the door, or rape her before they did, just to add to the thrill of the game and get revenge for wounding Bone Head Jimmy Gains and the killing by her husband of Rawlinson.

He stared at the flames roaring up to consume the building, and Heidi Strange. Unable to look, he closed his eyes and clenched his fists. Also, he realized he had begun to shake violently. What, in God's name, was he doing here, doing *this*? This wasn't *war*. All the books said men with honour fought wars, were chivalrous and magnanimous in victory, that to ride into battle was a brave and glorious thing to do. It was all a myth, a terrible deception.

The roar of a Colt nearby wrenched him out of his trauma. Dumbfounded, he saw Heidi Strange was falling to the hard-packed ground before the homestead, her back ablaze. Set on fire, she must have run from the building. Jaul was standing close by, smoking Colt in hand. Then he saw Kinder, clearly finished towing the remains of Henry Strange. He was now dismounted and standing in front of Heidi Strange's shrieking, writhing form, gun out, his face a mask of demonic pleasure. He began to pump lead into her until she screamed no more. And all the time Jaul was bawling at Kinder to stop shooting, saying he wanted to see the bitch burn, wanted to hear her holler. Zack Boles was beside Jaul, yelling his full agreement with the buck-toothed little bastard's sadistic wishes. But Kinder only grinned at them before turning once more to Henry Strange, who astoundingly, was still alive, though a bloody pulp.

Kinder giggled and drew his big knife. 'Jest one more leetle job,' he said.

He began moving towards Strange. Layton found he could but stare, aghast, as Kinder went to work with his blade while the others urged him on . . .

2

Felling trees half a mile down the creek from the homestead, Wolfgang Strange heard the harsh roaring of guns. One savage bang, then lots of them.

He stopped swinging his axe and stared through the drizzle.

Creeping dread began to grow in him. The seventeen-year-old's grey gaze hardened. There was news of the sacking of a town called Lawrence, in Kansas, by Quantrill. It filtered into the valley weeks ago. Rumours followed of harsh 'Orders' being passed in that new state in retaliation. And, surprisingly, the news finally seemed to do something to Pa. Uncharacteristically, he began to make it plain those 'Orders' must inevitably lead to something bad around here and soon.

Wolf pursed his lips. Well, he'd formed his own opinions on the state of things around the Strange household. They didn't agree with Pa's dogged, steadfast neutrality, but, out of respect, he remained silent regarding them. However, a week ago, Pa started carrying a gun . . .

At first Wolf found himself excited by the change, for Pa always said when a man took up a gun he immediately announced his intentions. But, in contradiction, Wolf discovered Pa's change of attitude soon began to disturb and worry *him*. He quickly realized youthful bravado was one thing when you didn't have to prove it, it was entirely another when you faced the reality.

Swallowing on his suddenly dry throat, he stared down the valley. The words just sprang from his lips, laced with disbelief. 'Ma? Pa?'

He started to pace forward, all the time staring towards the homestead. More vicious cracks of gunfire shattered the day's damp calm, then he heard faint screams. It had to be Ma. Stark sounds that split the cool, drizzly air, sending further daggers of anxiety coursing through him. Then he saw the black smoke start snaking up above the gaunt trees. He hardly realized he'd begun to run.

Once across the land he and Pa had cleared of trees, his boots now drummed heavily on the new wooden bridge they'd built to span the creek. In his anxious state the noise they made sounded like the drum of a death tattoo.

The bridge was the pride of this section of the valley. As they were able to afford it, Pa, Errol Blake, his two sons, Fred and Charlie — good neighbours — and himself built it during what free time they could make over the past two years. It now enabled Pa and himself to get across the creek to clear the rich ground there of scrub and timber; the work he was engaged on just now. Also, it gave access to a better road to get them into Beely, the town six miles down the valley.

Across the bridge he went off the track and sloshed his way through the trees by the creek to avoid taking time using the wide, rising loop in the trail they made to avoid the spring high water, though the water level was high enough now with the recent prolonged rain.

But, as soon as he started out across the soggy ground, he realized it was his youth and anxiety that was making him act crazy like this, going across this spongy, root-exposed ground instead of using the relatively puddle free road. But now embarked upon that course, it didn't deter him. His alarm just told him to run the shortest route, and that's what he was doing.

Then he slipped, crashed against some spring flood debris. The jolt spun his axe out of his hand. He watched in despair as it arced into the fast running water and was swallowed up. God damn! Pa had always said he was gawky as a day-old colt!

He scrambled up, began running

once more, but, within seconds, his foot hooked under a submerged root sending him floundering headlong, crashing into a thick, low-hanging branch. Stars flew across his vision, then blackness crowded down.

How long he lay there, out cold, he didn't know. As he opened his eyes the greyness of the day appeared once more to him. It took him a few moments to come to terms with where he was and what had happened to him. The chilly wetness against his back and face caused him to shiver. As he gained perception he realized he was lying on the soggy ground amongst the water-borne detritus of rotting branches under the live willows by the creek, brought down by previous flood water and jammed there. His head was thumping like the engine of a riverboat, battling its way upstream. Gingerly, he fingered the lump on his forehead.

Fighting the insistent feeling he should stay there awhile, he climbed to his feet and staggered to the muddy road. There was something urgent he had to do. Ma. Pa. He'd hardly begun running again when he heard the pounding of hooves coming from up trail, from the direction of the homestead. Before he could take any evasive action, the galloping riders came swinging around the bend. Mud-spattered, wild-eyed men whooping and waving their Colts and carbines. One he knew for sure: Mitch Layton, one-time neighbour. He got a good view of the other faces too. He found himself automatically etching their features into his memory as they bore down on him. Oddly, he had this sure conviction he would need to remember those brutish visages, seal them in his mind.

As they swept up on him he reacted spontaneously, for he gut-felt knew they were the men responsible for the gunfire and smoke at the homestead that had set him running. He launched himself at the first rider and grabbed hold of his right leg, wrapped around with red sheepskin leggings. With all his might he tried to pull the rider off his horse, though he hadn't an inkling of what he was going to do when he had done. The rider began cursing as he glared down at him, then he leaned over and tried to beat him off with his Colt Army. His face was an evil mask behind his fierce red beard.

'Git your damned hands off, you sonofabitch,' he bawled.

Wolf hung on, dragged along with the momentum of the running horse. Then he realized the man's Colt was booming, almost in his ear. The impact of something hitting him in the side of the head immediately sent streamers of white light exploding across his vision. There followed another crashing shot, another impact on his body. It caused him to let go and he found himself rolling over and over in the wet grass. Everything began going black again, no matter how he fought against it.

A snarl on his face exposing tobacco-stained teeth, Hetch Kinder halted his horse and kicked back towards the boy.

Towering over him he deliberately sighted his Colt on the bleeding youth, lying unconscious in the sodden trailside grass. Mitch Layton, Kelsy Jaul, Bone Head Jimmy Gains and Zack Boles reined up their lathered mounts around him. It was Mitch Layton who cut his horse across his line of fire.

'That's enough, damn it,' Layton bawled. 'He's dead. Can't yuh see?'

Kinder turned his maddened, menacing glare. 'Git outa the way.'

Zack Boles urged his big bay forward. 'Jesus, Hetch, the kid's already funeral material. Why waste lead?'

Then Bone Head Jimmy Gains growled, 'Damn it, Hetch, it's me needs fixin', not the boy. Let's git.' White-faced with the strain of pain, he grimaced and stared down and grasped at his bloody, birdshot damaged leg.

Layton almost felt Kinder's wrathful stare as it swung across them all. Kinder's killing urges seemed to be awful, conflicting forces, wrestling within him. His knuckles showed stark white around his big Colt as he strained against the clear urge to pull the trigger. Layton couldn't believe it was the waste of lead that was staying Kinder's trigger finger, nor could he believe it was compassion. Kinder hadn't got it in him.

However, after moments of what seemed to be a gathering madness that threatened to explode in a frenzy of violence, Kinder appeared to take hold of himself. With a string of oaths he hoisted his yellow slicker and rammed his Colt into the holster underneath. He snarled and glared around him. 'God damn, what's git into you sonsofbitches? He's jest a lousy Reb brat.' Then he turned. Layton caught his murderous stare. 'An' you, mister . . . jest don't git in my way agin, you hear me? You're through with this outfit from now.'

Layton returned the glare. 'Thet suits me fine.'

Kinder hunched forward in the saddle, his eyes sparking anger, then, viciously, he turned his horse and lashed it into motion and thundered off across the bridge. 'Let's git!'

Streaming past Layton, the rest gathered in behind Kinder.

★   ★   ★

Wolf realized it was Errol Blake's calm gaze he was staring into as he came out of his second bout of unconsciousness. He felt the cold rain falling steadily on to his face. He was aware of pain, too, but behind it there was still something urgent buzzing in the back of his mind — something he had to do as fast as he could. He struggled to get up, but vivid agony exploded through him and he cried out, harshly.

He felt Errol Blake's big hand easing him down. 'Try an' rest easy, boy. You're hurt real bad.'

But Wolf found this insistent urge wouldn't let him 'rest'. There was something he had to do. It was a compelling, drumming in his head. He — had — to — get — to — the — homestead. Something was wrong there.

He tried to get up again. 'Ma an' Pa,' he said.

Errol Blake eased him down, nodded patiently. 'Jest as soon as we've git you fixed up, boy.'

Now feeling cold and unable to stop himself shivering, Wolf stared around him. Fred and Charlie, Errol Blake's two boys were sitting in the back of the Blake wagon, staring at him. Jed Stringer and his three boys from the homestead four miles south, down the valley, were gathered on and around their wagon.

Gritting his teeth, Wolf reared up once more, pushing against Errol Blake's hand. 'I gotta git home. I got to see what's happened to my folks.'

Errol Blake's look was furtive, as if he didn't want to meet his stare. 'It jest ain't pretty, Wolf,' he said. 'It can wait. We got to git you to the doc.'

'Heed him, boy,' Jed Stringer said. He was sitting tall and dripping wet on the seat of his buckboard. 'I'll tell you straight, son, if we don't git you to the doctor in Beely purty quick we gonna have more buryin' to do.'

A fierce stab of pain caused Wolf to put his hand to his head. Ever since he had come to his skull had throbbed with almost unbearable intensity. His hand came away wet with blood, despite the makeshift wrapping he felt was on the wound. Pain racked his chest, too. Staring down he gathered his wounds had been roughly doctored and dressed and his bloodsoaked homespun shirt replaced. Trying to control his shivering he reached for Errol Blake's coat lapel and grasped it. He bored his stare into the homesteader's worried look.

'I gotta see what's happened, sir,' he said. 'Got to fix it in my mind. You gotta understand that.'

Errol Blake stared at him, long and hard. 'But, boy, it ain't gonna do any good. We gotta git you into Beely like Jed said.'

Wolf gripped harder, urgently. 'I got to do it.'

A little helplessly, Errol Blake looked at Jed Stringer. Stringer shrugged and said, 'If the boy wants it. We'll jest hev' to chance the rest. He's allus been a strong boy. Mebbe he's up to it.'

Blake appeared to deliberate on the consequences of the decision a moment or two longer, then he firmed his lips and turned to his two sons. 'Help me git Wolf into the back of the buckboard.'

As Wolf sighed his silent thanks Fred and Charlie came off the rig at a fast pace. Wolf felt strangely at ease to find they had come with their Pa. It had been Wolf, Fred and Charlie for nigh on fifteen years — playing around, hunting in the woods, working around each others' farms, doing every kind of growing up in the back country a boy can do with good friends.

'Easy, boys,' Errol Blake said. 'Don't

want to do more damage.'

Wolf felt his friends' hands gently lift him. Even so, pain snarled in every limb. He gritted his teeth, but he couldn't prevent his breath hissing through them as he attempted to hold his agony down. They began making for the back of the buckboard. He didn't want to be there. 'Like to be seated up front, sir,' he said. 'Gotta be sittin' to see it.' In his gut he knew there was something awful up there at the homestead.

Errol stared at him, then nodded. 'As you wish, boy,' he said. 'But it's gonna hurt real bad, I reckon.'

Once settled, Errol Blake geed up the horse. Immediately, the movement sent waves of pain flooding through Wolf. Seated beside him, Fred Blake took time to take off his coat and put it around him, then, holding the reins in one hand, but his free arm around his wide shoulders. Wolf recognized, in his way, Fred was making his effort to try comfort him, help him fight the pain

41

and trying to protect him from the worst jolts of the uneven road. Meantime, dour-looking Jed Stringer was calling to his big dray horse. When he got it moving he pulled his long flat wagon in behind them, his three boys sitting wet and grim-faced in the back.

Five minutes later they were at the homestead — what was left of it. Wolf stared with bleak eyes. Barn, outbuildings, house . . . black, smoking ruins, hissing in the steadily falling rain, a few flames still spurting up occasionally, as if in defiance. Ma, he saw, was lying headlong in front of the house, the shot-gun kept behind Pa's chair in the parlour a few inches in front of her, obviously jolted from her grasp. As he stared, Wolf felt he wanted to vomit. Ma's back was crisped, her head blown apart. She lay in a great pool of her own blood. Pa, he now saw, was close by. He was hardly recognizable; his face and body just a bloody pulp. But, worst of all, somebody had cut off his penis and stuffed it into his mouth, as if to show their contempt for him and to underscore the obscenity of what had happened here. What perverted scum could have done this?

He gasped, turned away. Errol Blake held him, as if to share his pain, help him through it. After moments he said, 'Reckon we can git you to Beely now, son.'

Hardly hearing Mr Blake's plea, Wolf felt he wanted to cry, but no tears would come — just a cold, creeping, iron resolve manifested itself slowly within him; a resolve to avenge this atrocity, a decision to hunt the perpetrators to the ends of the earth, if need be.

He stared at Errol Blake. 'There's the buryin',' he said.

'We'll see to it,' said Jed Stringer, sitting the seat of the big flat, gaunt and wet nearby, his three boys, Nate, John and Ethan staring, white-faced, at the ruins around them. Jed added, 'Git yourself better, boy. Then, from here on, we got big work to do in this here war. We've done had our side picked fer us.'

Wolf nodded slowly. 'I guess so,' he said. The words fell bitterly from his lips.

Even as he spoke, he sensed a silent, deadly resolve was descending upon all the men and youths sitting there. Though some in the valley had marched off to war early, most had wanted no part of the conflict because there were families to rear, stock to tend, crops to grow and, for the much more mundane reason, they couldn't decide which side to fight on. Now, it seems, as Jed Stringer had said, their minds had been made up for them. Like it or not.

Wolf blinked, his eyes filled with cold hate. 'Guess I'll see the doc now, Mr Blake, if you don't mind.'

3

East Texas, Early May 1866.

Weak with exhaustion, Wolf crouched hidden in the willow breaks between the river and the trail. He was almost out of the hilly, wooded country now. Silhouetted in the early morning sun, barely a hundred yards away, Captain Fenger and his Red Legs jingled past, single file, their horses steamy and head-bowed — played out, like the men riding them. Grim, hard men who, up until now, had been hell-bent on hounding down the last remnants of the bunch Wolf ran with, long since dubbed the Strange Gang.

It gave Wolf a feeling of malevolent comfort to see the bedraggled state of his pursuers. They had been as dogged in their hunting as he and the gang had been in their flight and bloody skirmishing to deny them of the glory to be had from the capture and death of Wolf Strange's Raiders. But his own thoughts were bitter: when were they going to quit?

He scrubbed at the two weeks' growth of dark beard matting his stubborn chin and compressed beartrap lips. He knew at this moment he looked much older than his twenty years. Maybe now he and Fred Blake, wounded and hidden in the willows back yonder, would be left alone for a spell; maybe, between them, they would be able to make enough ground to lose themselves in this vast Texas hinterland.

Wolf rubbed his sore eyes. But God he was tired, wasted down, sick of this continual hounding. He knew he and Fred only had a short respite before those sonsofbitches would be on their trail again. It seemed a lifetime had gone by since he had stared at the ravaged corpses of his parents on that bleak November morning of '63, before he had finally passed out through loss of blood and the Blakes had taken him into Beely to have the doc treat his wounds.

After a cursory look at his injuries, the sawbones said he gave him little chance of surviving them, but he'd do what he could. The physician further announced much would depend on his constitution. Thinking on it now, Wolf shook his head, even allowed himself a grim smile. Well, that young body of his had proved to be in fine condition and had healed fast.

Meantime, holed up in Beely, Fred and Charlie Blake, like true friends, despite constant Union patrols skirmishing through the area stuck with him, protected him, while news repeatedly came in that Order 11 was still being carried out to the letter right along the border. It was reported over-zealous Kansas state militias, Jayhawkers and Red Legs were on a campaign of burning and killing, making a wasteland of the whole area.

How Beely escaped the torch was a miracle.

Meantime, while Fred and Charlie Blake watched over him, Errol Blake and Jed Stringer, and other men affected by the ruthless purge, gathered their familes — got them to whatever safety they could find, be it with relatives or sympathizers in safer areas.

Then came the day Wolf found himself healed up. With Errol Blake and his boys, Jed Stringer's brood and other run-out homesteaders, they swept out to take revenge — raiding into Kansas, seeking out anybody they thought were taking part in the border bloodletting. To finance their activities, Wolf planned daring bank raids and attacks on Union supply trains. Overnight he became a man — thrown as he was into the bloody, vicious, often deadly, silent war he became embroiled in.

As did the men he rode with, he soon discovered he possessed natural abilities of leadership and an uncanny knack of understanding and executing the hit-and-run tactics needed for the covert warfare they were engaged in. In short time he was nominated to be their leader. There followed nearly two years of savage, no-holds-barred skirmishing — fought out on lonely, wooded hillsides, across deserted fields or holed up in ruined, desolated settlements.

Lee's surrender at Appomattox Courthouse, though deplored and unrecognized by some Southern factions, suggested hope for many — a return to peace and a chance to rebuild their lives. But Wolf and his men soon found it was not for them. The Strange Gang was top priority; branded a no-good band of cutthroat pillagers. That they had been fighting for a cause as well as survival didn't enter into it.

And, rumour came, they weren't on their own. Bitterness between the states of Kansas and Missouri still ran deep. In certain lonely places, news came of other bands like their own, hounded and hungry, were being lured into captivity only to be butchered, officially or unofficially, after they had voluntarily given up their arms. Few records were kept; maybe the real authorities never knew, Wolf decided. But many old scores were being settled, in full. Victims were buried in lonely, unmarked graves, their deaths and the manner of it, remaining unproven or ignored. For sure it seemed the ruthless, gore-laden tactics practised by William Clark Quantrill, Bloody Bill Anderson and their ilk had long ago set the seal on the ultimate fate of many Missouri irregulars, when the North-South dispute was brought to its final, bloody conclusion.

Shivering in the early morning cold, Wolf watched with predatory stare, as the Red Legs finally disappeared into an arroyo a mile or so from his position. Six days had elapsed since he'd known the blessed respite of a long, deep sleep. There had been only brief naps grabbed between moments of high anxiety and desperate skirmishing as they had run for their lives.

Now Wolf's haggard features sagged and became rancorous as he remembered. Last week, even after last ditch pleadings with them to continue to tough it out, Errol and Charlie Blake decided to go in. Wolf raised dark brows. For sure, it was rumoured in the settlements they'd passed through recently, there was talk of an amnesty for those who gave themselves up and promised to be Reconstructed — that is recognize the Union and vow allegiance to it. Wolf pushed his chisel chin into a grim line, the tired lines on his grubby, hollow face setting even deeper. He had to admit Errol and Charlie's bid would have been fine . . . if it had worked out. But, from the start, he'd known it wouldn't.

Remorseless hate consumed Wolf. With trepidation, he viewed the surrender proceedings from cover. On a green lea, in a gap in the woods, Errol and Charlie were interrogated, given a mockery of a trial, before being strung up like criminals, kicking until they died. Their corpses were then subjected to the final humiliation. They were left hanging there to rot with REBEL MURDERERS scrawled on some card and tied around Errol's neck.

Now he stared at Fred Blake, hollow-eyed and hidden in the willows close by. Fred was leaner than a bear-trapped cougar and waiting to die. He went to him.

'Reckon we've seen the last o' Fenger for a spell,' he said.

Fred raised pain-harried eyes. 'You figure?'

Wolf nodded. 'I reckon this is a chance to git ourselves outa this.'

Fred stared up. 'You reckon?'

Wolf kept his stare on his friend. 'You know I gotta leave you fer a spell, Fred,' he said. 'You know we need food, horses.'

His friend's brows arched above his brilliant blue eyes as he looked up. 'So, God damn it — ain't you gone yet?'

The effort of talking made Fred

cough wearily. A new trickle of blood began to seep out of the corner of his mouth, replacing the one Wolf had cleaned up minutes ago.

Wolf fiddled with his neckerchief. 'You know I'll be back.'

Fred smiled weakly, exposing blood-stained teeth before more coughing erupted more blood. When he recovered, he said, his face as serious as a blue norther, 'You crazy?' He cut air with his hand. 'Chris'sake, keep on goin', Wolf. Save yuhself. Yuh know as well as me I'm played out. No regrets. Accept thet an git.'

Wolf stared. Somehow, he felt cheated. 'Well, to hell with that,' he said. 'I ain't havin' you give up on me after carryin' you fer two days. You stay close now while I scout out the land. We'll see this through, bet on it.'

That brought a harsh laugh from Fred, but it soon faded to a grimace as pain hit. He said, 'Hell, Wolf, I ain't about to go nowhere, am I? You know thet as well as me.'

'I do.' Then Wolf pointed a severe finger. 'So think what we got to look forward to, will yuh? A good life, a long life. Meantime, jest stop talkin' like yuh beat.'

Fred's stare rounded. 'Thet how it sounded?'

Wolf shuffled and sniffed, as if resentfully. 'Yuh know damn well.'

However, he knew as well as Fred it was a deadly charade they were playing here and it was screwing him up inside to have to, forcing pain and anguish into him when he thought he had got that kind of thing tamed — thought that he had forced himself not to *feel* any more. But, resist as he might he could not stop himself remembering the long summer days he, Fred and Charlie had played as kids along the creek. Anything from pirates to Indians. His gut knotted again. Damn it, it wasn't right. Here Fred was, just passed his nineteenth birthday — a birthday that should have been celebrated before his father and his brother Charlie had gone in to be Reconstructed. Trying hard not to show his misery he knelt and supported Fred's head and brought up his canteen. Though he was now shivering badly Fred gulped water hungrily.

'I'll leave the canteen with you an' what bread we have,' Wolf said. 'Got to be a ranch, homestead of some sort around here. Ideal country fer thet. Then, damn it, we'll have you on yuh feet in no time.'

Fred nodded, grinned his ghastly, bloody grin. 'Yeah,' he said. He looked up, serious now. 'Those sonsofbitches . . . they *really* gone?'

Wolf put down the canteen. 'Fer a while, I guess.'

Fred sighed and lay back. 'Yeah, fer a while.' Defeat now dulled his once bright, laughing blue eyes. 'But, hell, they jest don't let up, Wolf, do'ey?' he said. 'Jest keep comin'.'

Wolf pursed his lips. 'Sure seems thet way. But neither do we, Fred, an' I figure *they're* beat up real bad right now. They've gone slinkin' off. We've played hell with 'em last couple o' days, though we did lose our hosses along the way. Thing is we jest got to keep toughin' 'em out. Reckon at the moment they're headin' fer some settlement or other — top up their supplies, rest up a day or two. I reckon this could be our first real chance to give 'em the slip.'

Fred's gaze turned up again, hope flashing momentarily. 'Yeah. God damn, we'll be long gone, huh, boy?'

Wolf nodded. 'Hell, long gone,' he said. 'You bet.'

Without another word he crept out of the willows. In the less densely foliated part of the creek he looked at the broad bands of trees that hugged each side of this Texas stream for as far as he could see, then, scrambling up the river bank, he gazed upon rolling, seemingly endless, grassland, broken up by stands of trees, which suggested other water sources further ahead.

Nothing moved out there which

could suggest men had been left behind by Fenger to trap them. Though relaxed further by his findings he felt the unwelcome, early morning sun warming his back, promising yet another searing hot, draining day. But still, the larks and other birds were singing their cheerful tunes. It caused a poignant, bitter-sweet thread of remembrance to run through him for a moment. There was a time when he had idly lain in the grass with Fred and Charlie and . . .

He shook himself out of his nostalgia. It did no good to hark back. It stirred too many ghosts, too many memories.

The eye scout over, he returned to the creek, bathed his face and took a long drink of water from it, then stared once more at the pure blue sky and drew in lungfuls of clean air, keeping his gaze off the already brassy sun beginning to glare down on everything. Then, topping the steep river bank once more, he glanced back briefly. Fred Blake was well hidden in the brakes, his guns arranged around him and within easy reach. If you didn't know where to look you'd miss Fred by a mile he thought optimistically.

Seeing him looking, Fred grinned, waved weakly. Wolf swallowed on a dry throat. He knew instinctively this could be the last he would ever see of Fred alive, but he could still hope, and would do. Somehow, he would do his damnedest to get back to Fred, then it would be west, always west. Texas had been for the CS of A. There must be a deal of sympathy around here still . . . somewhere.

Growing more sick with the fever in him, he began walking. He'd hardly gone twenty yards beyond the low ridge when the crack of a Colt set his heart racing and his gut snarling up. He didn't have to focus his gaze to search the area for hostile riders, for he instinctively knew what had happened and what he had hoped against.

He tottered back down the long bank and blundered through the willows. Gunsmoke was still coming from Fred's mouth into which he had put the cap-and-ball Colt Navy and blown the top of his head clean off.

Wolf clasped his hands together over him, allowing his intense remorse to well up, before anger replaced it. It was all such a monstrous waste. 'Damn you, Fred,' he raged, 'we could have made it! I promised you we would!' But he knew Fred had called a spade a spade, done his level best to make sure that *he*, his friend, survived by removing himself from his strong feelings of responsibility. Bitterly digesting this, Wolf stared at his dead comrade. It had to be like this. And no true friend could do more, but it didn't make the tragedy any easier to bear.

The digging of the shallow grave with his Bowie knife took him until mid-morning, leaving him drenched with sweat. He was so damned weak himself. He said a few words over the mound of earth, pushed in the willow cross he had fashioned. Then he filled the canteen, hoisted the strap on to his shoulder. Presently, drained of all emotion, he began to walk. As he did, the sun seemed to grow stronger, become a constant fierce ball above him, nauseating him, attacking him, making him feel there was no moisture left in him, that what there was was constantly being sucked out.

The third hour into his staggering walk he drank the last of his water. Under his burning feet the grass was brown, coarse and wiry, continually scorching him through the gaping holes in his worn out boots. His two Army Colts, one in the cavalry holster and one in his belt, felt like ton weights about his bony hips. The long Henry rifle he owned was hot and sticky and burning in his hand. But he would not give them up, even if it meant dropping dead with them still in his belt and in his hand. He'd go down ready to fight, choose what. There were other incentives, too. He had dead friends to avenge and the murderous savagery inflicted on his Ma and Pa to redress. *He had to live.*

Half an hour later, he paused on the top of a swell in the land to wipe the moisture from his brow and stare at the vast, endless, burning land, looking for anything that suggested sanctuary. But when he saw the mound of bare earth in the shallow, mile-wide basin way down at the bottom of the slope before him he couldn't bring himself to believe it. It must be one of those damned mirages he'd read about and seen pictures of in one of Pa's few books. Things just didn't happen like that, not to him anyway.

He passed a trembling hand across his brow, trying to focus on the dugout. But it was real enough. It stuck up out of the yellow land like a sore thumb. Sods and soil excavated from the dug hole was piled up around it, to give more height. It stood on a rise of ground. It had been built by a small creek coming from God knew where which already looked to be drying up. There was a mass of rocks miles in the distance. Maybe it sprang up out of those . . .

Seeing it almost caused him to sob with relief. The fact was, though, for some time he had been seeing groups of cows grazing the range. That should have told him something, but he'd missed it; he was too far gone. Then, again, it was not an uncommon sight to see in this big land. When they had first encountered them, Errol Blake speculated the years of war must have caused herds to run wild and multiply, the range being empty of the men who had left to fight a war.

Now he saw a pole corral of sorts standing fifty yards or so from the soddy. He could see three horses were in it. From the tin smokestack poking out of the top of the dugout, smoke was flattening across the earth roof, driven by the scorching breeze coming towards him. The smell of burning buffalo chips and timber engaged his nostrils. He'd discovered they had a odour all their own.

He tottered forward, his cry of relief emerging as a croaking through dry, cracked lips. The soddy seemed to be moving like water before his eyes. His found he couldn't focus on it properly, the eroding of weeks of privation, even on his strong body, had been so great, so debilitating. But, coming up to it, his joy became short-lived. The familiar metallic click of a rifle being cocked brought him to a stop. He found he resented the noise greatly. Texas was supposed to be for the Confederacy, God damn it!

'Stay there now, y'hear?' came the call.

He tried to focus on the woman who uttered the warning. She was framed in the crude doorway. She was in faded and worn blue gingham. She looked young, younger than himself, but her face had the marks of a hard life, making her — like himself — look stronger and older than her apparent years. Her raven dark hair was straggly and unkempt, but, he noticed, the Volcanic rifle she held was convincingly steady in her hands.

'I need food, water, ma'am,' he rasped, the effort hurting his throat. 'A horse.'

'Yeah, thet's clear.' But there was no feeling in her flat tone.

'You oblige me?'

'Why should I?'

He fought to keep erect, but the woman began to lose shape before his wavering gaze. He half-realized he could stop his dogged walking now — his eyes fixed on some landmark in the far distance so he would keep walking straight. It seemed now that he had found some sort of sanctuary, his body could let go, divorce itself from his steel will — the will that had driven him to keep going for so long.

'Because . . . ' he said. He stared stupidly at her. He didn't know whether to laugh or cry, but knew he'd do neither. 'Because I'm jest played out, ma'am.'

Then it felt as though his body was crumbling like dried-out soil, disintegrating and falling to the ground. He had no power to stop it.

4

Roused from sleep, Wolf quickly realized it was people talking that was dragging him out of his deep slumber. Coming rapidly awake the words he heard were not good and they caused extreme apprehension to spurt through him.

'I'm Captain Fenger, ma'am.' There was a pause. 'My men and I are on the trail of a killer. Has anybody called in here or passed by within the last day or so?'

'Till you showed up, ain't bin nobody 'round here fer two weeks.' That was the woman.

Coming to full alertness Wolf immediately appreciated he was in the dugout, on a bed of sorts; that he was naked; that he was bathed in sweat because of the oppressive heat trapped inside the dwelling. Making it worse, the small oven against the far wall was lit and a pot of aromatic stew was simmering on it. The meaty smell of it hungered him. Now he noticed a worn blanket that had obviously covered him had fallen on to the earth floor — a floor covered with buffalo pelts. The only light illuminating the place was what came from the small doorway. He saw the woman was framed in it, blocking out most of the outside view. However, he did catch glimpses of riders arranged in a half-circle before the dwelling. He noticed the Volcanic rifle was in the woman's hands. It was clear she was prepared to use it. He looked around. He saw his own Henry, propped in the corner at the foot of the bed. He grasped it, hoping the woman hadn't unloaded it.

'You live here alone, ma'am?' Fenger was saying.

The woman said, 'My man's in the house, sick.'

Fenger said, 'We would like to talk to him. We have questions to ask him, identifications to make. We've got certain matters to clear up.'

As if to challenge them, the woman tilted her head. 'Can come in if you like. Have to tell you he's got the cholera, though.'

The woman inviting them in caused Wolf's stomach to clench up, but the talk of plague brought an instant swell of relief. It was a killer ace, well played.

Clearly startled, Fenger said, '*Cholera*, ma'am?'

The woman said, 'That's right.'

Talk was now being bantered to and fro outside, then Fenger said, 'My men and I are of the opinion you are lyin', ma'am.'

The woman immediately made ready with the rifle. Wolf reckoned the move would have been melodramatic had it had not been so obviously full of deadly intent. 'Now, I've heard tell men are prepared to kill fer less than bein' accused o' that. What makes you think a woman ain't? You got an invite: you takin' it up or not?'

Obviously flustered, Fenger said, 'How d'you know it's the cholera?'

'I know right enough,' the woman said. 'I've survived it; nursed my family while most of them died of it.'

There was another uncertain pause, more talk, before Fenger said, 'I see, ma'am. That does give you knowledge of it.'

'Damned right,' the woman said.

Once more gruff responses began bouncing to and fro between the gathered men. Wolf came to the conclusion considerable of the riders were now expressing an urgent wish to be gone, *pronto*.

Fenger soon proved he was made of sterner stuff. He said, 'You act as though you are nervous, ma'am. I would suggest you are fabricating because you have been exposed to the man we are hunting. Perhaps he called on you, took what he needed and warned you not to talk to anybody on pain of death. Was it like that?'

The woman said, 'Told you. Nobody's

been by fer two week.'

'He's a tall man,' said Fenger. 'Young. He may have been wearing some Confederate grey. He has a Rebel hat for sure. He goes by the name of Wolf Strange. The Wolf being short for Wolfgang.'

Framed in the small doorway the woman made an impatient move, craned forward aggressively. 'Damn it, is your hearin' none too good, mister? I said *nobody.*'

Fenger said, in the same monotone, 'He's a murderer, ma'am. We have been ordered by the Federal authorities in Kansas to hunt him down for crimes perpetrated in that state.'

The woman said, 'Since when have Red Legs been the law?' She did not attempt to hide her contempt.

Wolf tensed. Damn it, she was going out of her way to rock the boat. Following her scornful reply a steely resonance entered Fenger's reply. 'Ma'am, we have a job to do. I am doing my best to be reasonable.'

70

To Wolf's relief, the woman appeared to relax a little. She sniffed. 'Well, maybe you are. But, like I keep tellin' you, he ain't here. If he had called he'd have been given short shrift, like I'm givin' you.' She waved the rifle impatiently. 'Now, you goin' to look in on my husband, or ain't you? I git chores to do, duds full o' shit to wash.'

After a pause, several whoops and raucous guffaws came from the gathered Red Legs. But Wolf froze once more. *What the hell was the crazy woman doing — inviting them in . . . again*!

As if unmoved by her abrupt vulgarity, Fenger said, 'Well, you don't mince your words, ma'am.' There was no hint of humour in *his* voice. A pause followed. It suggested to Wolf, Fenger was deliberating on her challenge then he said, 'All right, men, column of twos.' Another pause. 'One thing, ma'am . . . we'll water our horses at the creek, fill our canteens. If that's agreeable.'

'You will anyway, whether it's agreeable or not,' the woman said.

Once more a Red Leg hooted his glee. 'Jeeesus! Seems to me we're in Texas, a' right, boys. Spiky as a porcupine, this li'l lady. Maybe we ought to teach her what a woman's place in life truly is. Appears she's plumb fergot.' Ribald laughs and vulgar agreement greeted the proposal. Adding to it, somebody warbled, 'Yer know, boys, I ain't had a woman since . . . well, God knows when. So, how about it? Shall we see what's under her drawers — if she's got any on, thet is. Ain't much call fer such do-das out here, I reckon.'

Another more cautious individual said, 'If they got the cholera in there, count me out, boys.'

Fenger rapped, clearly angry, 'That'll be enough, men. Remember, you are under military law. I'll have no such behaviour while I'm in command.'

'We ought to damn well kill her, the mouthy bitch,' a man said. 'I'm sick an' tired o' mouthy bitches, sick an' tired of this here damned country, sick an' tired o' chasin' thet damned sonofabitch Strange.' As if to find an excuse to grouse some more, or to get at the woman, he growled, 'Your man fight in the war, woman?'

The answer came quick as a flash. 'Texas Brigade.' As she said the words the woman moved the Volcanic to her shoulder. 'And, in case you're wonderin', I c'n shoot, too. An' if you git any more funny ideas, I won't take you all, but I'll take some.'

A rider said, irately, 'Why, damn your big ass, you really are askin' fer it.'

'Leave it, Johnson,' snapped Fenger, a fierce edge to his voice. After a pause he added, calmly, 'That was a fine outfit, ma'am. My compliments to your husband. We will leave you to your sad duties. Good day.'

That caused a trickle like ice water to crawl down Wolf's back. Suspicion reared up in him. This was all too easy, but he relaxed a little as he heard the jingle of harness, the creak of leather and the patter of horses' hooves moving away from the dugout. Then, in the distance, he heard horses pawing the water while drinking their fill, then he listened to the heavy drum of receding hooves beating the baked earth until there was silence.

It was only then the woman relaxed, lowered her rifle, turned and came into the dugout. As she did, Wolf put the Henry down and drew the blanket about him, suddenly aware of his nudity. When she saw he was looking at her, her return look was dull, indifferent.

'You're finally awake, huh?' she said.

'You covered for me, lady. Why? I'm nothin' to you.'

'You're right. You're nothin' to me.' Then she hunched her narrow shoulders, walked across the dugout and propped the Volcanic in the far right corner. 'I've had troubles in the war of my own. I got a helping hand once. I

74

just had an urge to help you. Can you believe that?'

He studied her pale face. He saw little emotion in it. 'I'd like to. Opinions about me ain't been too flatterin' of late, an' mostly believed.'

She moved to the rough table in the centre of the floor space and sat on one of the crude chairs. 'Who's Heidi?' she said.

The question was so blunt it made him start. It was a long time since he had last heard that name spoken and it roused instant, painful memories. 'My mother. How come you know about her?'

The woman shrugged again. 'You've been fevered fer three days. Pa, Ma, Henry, Heidi, Errol, Fred, Charlie. You talked a lot, swore a lot.' She added tonelessly, 'She's dead, ain't she.' That was a statement.

Surprised he'd been out so long and had revealed so much about himself Wolf said, 'Yes.' He studied her plain features and ragged blue gingham dress. 'Still don't explain why you covered fer me. Like the man said, I'm Wolf Strange' — he reared up, tried to look scary — 'badman.'

Unimpressed, her grey gaze studied him. 'We have a number of men comin' through on the run. The men followin' them always claim they're bad. Now, I've never believed all Confederate soldiers are criminals.'

Wolf raised dark brows. 'An' in thet belief you'd be right. But the difference with me is I was a Missouri raider, ma'am. In the opinion of most Kansans we are jest about the lowest thing on God's earth.'

She began stirring the stewpot on the stove. 'Heard that m'self,' she said. 'Well, you don't look a murderer to me.'

'An' I ain't,' he said, levelling his stare on to her. 'Nor were the men I rode with. We were in a war, jest like everbody else. When we got shot at, we shot back. Yeah, there was lootin' an' such, but I never took part in thet until late. We were starvin'. We got no pay. We had to git money for cartridges somehow. We had to forage for food to eat. We had to *survive*. That said, 'bout me not lookin' a killer, you shouldn't judge men's characters solely on appearances. I've known the most innocent-looking of blue-eyed boys turn out to be the evilist bein's there ever was.'

Her grey eyes probed him, a hint of amusement in them. 'You speechify regular?'

Slightly embarrassed, he offered her a wry grin and felt his cheeks heat up. 'Not as a rule, ma'am.' Then his curiosity got the better of him. 'Was your man really in the Texas Brigade?'

Her mouth corners turned up and she smiled, blooming her face, taking away the tiredness in it. 'You like thet idea?' she said.

'I'm told that was a fine outfit.'

She raised dark, shapely brows. 'Well, I got no man. Jest figured what I said might git the leader o' thet trash thinkin' like he did — respectin' other fightin' units, even if they were the enemy. I've met up with thet before. An' it appeared to me he weren't like the others.'

This time Wolf allowed himself a cold, cynical smile. 'There you go agin,' he said. 'Well, I'll tell you straight out, he's like the others a' right. A killer jest believing he's right in what he does. What he is, is a real trained military man . . . with orders. Lucky fer them, an' you, your crazy bluff worked. I had my rifle cocked. There could have been a lot o' blood spilled here jest now. You see, ma'am, I got nothin' to lose.'

She stared. 'So, don't thet make you a killer, too, like they say?' She clearly resented his criticism of her actions. 'Mister, my lyin' jest now got you outa the shit.'

The coarseness of her remark — to *him* — shocked him. He'd never met a woman like this before. All the women he had been brought up with hadn't used that kind of talk and would have been totally revolted by its use. He wanted to believe such talk didn't fit her, either; wanted to believe hard times had made her crude — hard situations in a man's world in which she'd had to give as good, or better, than she got. Another thing: who the hell was he to judge anybody?

He looked at her narrowly. For some crazy reason he felt protective towards her and that couldn't be either, things the way they were. He said, 'Don't you think you're takin' a mighty big chance, livin' out here on your own?'

Her grey stare was quick and searching before she lifted her chin defiantly. 'Ain't alone. My cousin's about. He and four other men are gatherin' a herd to take to Sedalia. He figures to make enough money outa the scheme to fix himself up with a real spread then gather an' take more herds to meet the railways bein' pushed across Kansas. Heard tell the North's cryin' out fer beef.' She looked away, as if to hide that she might be lying. 'He'll be back . . . anytime now, so don't git ideas.'

He rubbed at the fortnight's growth of beard covering his cleft chin. 'So, you lived out here long, ma'am?'

'Not long.'

She turned from stirring the stew and gazed at him. Beads of sweat were standing out on her broad forehead. Constantly, she wafted the flies away from her face — the flies causing the incessant buzz within the dwelling. Patches of perspiration showed through her threadbare gingham dress. This was a hell of a place to bring a woman, he thought. But he saw a deep, stubborn determination was built into her angular features. He guessed that strength had been there some time; guessed she intended to use that obstinate streak to fight for her rightful place in this hard land, no matter what.

She pouted. 'Come from Missouri. All my folks were killed in the raidin' an' I was left to beg, or pick up work an' feed any way I could. I did plenty I ain't proud of. But a hungry belly knows little pride, or has little conscience. When my cousin found out my plight he took me on an' brought me out here, after he'd done fightin' in the war. I'm real beholden to him. I judge him to be a fine man.'

Wolf nodded. 'He sounds like real kinfolk, fer sure. He around right now?'

'I tol' you he's around, didn't I?' she said, but she diverted her gaze again. Wolf figured, despite her recent hard times she still found it difficult to hide even white lies.

'He know about me?' he said.

'Not yet,' she said. She lifted her chin. 'An' he ain't likely to either. Guess you'll be leavin' soon, bein' who you are an' knowin' you have men chasin' you.'

'They've bin doin' thet fer months,' he said. 'You say I've been fevered fer three days?'

She nodded. 'I done the best I could fer you. You were in a real bad condition.' Now her gaze studied him.

'I guess you ought to know: my cousin fought with the Jayhawkers fer a while.'

He straightened immediately, tension building immediately. 'He *what?*'

She stared back defiantly, resentfully. 'I tol' you because I don't want to see him killed, or you, an' thet's why I want you to git. Fer me the war's over an' I figure it is fer my cousin. But you never know. Time men fergot warrin' an' took up the peace.'

Wolf couldn't prevent his lips curling into a bitter sneer. 'Jest now you learnt some men ain't allowed to take up the peace. An' there are some things a man can never fergit.'

She looked at him. He thought he saw a wisdom in her that shouldn't be in one so young. 'Never's a long time, Wolf Strange,' she said after moments. 'Jest what you done back there thet was so bad?'

He shrugged. 'Fer some I fought on the wrong side, in the wrong way.'

She cocked her head on one side. 'You favour Quantrill?'

Wolf raised his dark brows. 'I had a view once, but Pa kinda wanted us to stay out of the fightin'.' He glanced at her. 'He had strong Quaker views. However, after what happened at Lawrence . . . ' Wolf looked down and fiddled with the blanket he held tightly around his nakedness. 'Well, no, ma'am, I did *not* favour Quantrill.'

'Yet you became a guerrilla, a marauder.'

'There were other, bigger reasons fer doin' thet an' I have no regrets about it.' He got up. The talk was painful and getting him nowhere. 'Now, ma'am, I really could do with restin' up fer a few days. Your cousin . . . he be away long, you reckon?'

She fussed self-consciously with her worn dress. 'He has four men with him. Jest comes ridin' in unexpected. Could be back any time.'

She didn't convince him as being a very good liar. He said, 'Could be, I guess. But is it likely?'

He thought he saw a tinge of colour

come to her cheeks. Indecision was certainly there. It was clear she wasn't entirely sure of his 'intentions' and was going on instinct. 'Cousin figured he'd be out three weeks. Left me stores enough fer thet. Only two weeks gone.' She took time out to beat at the flies that buzzed constantly in the dugout. 'So, figure it out fer yerself . . . though he could be back, like I said.'

He felt she seemed less sure she wanted him to go now. 'I could do a few chores around here,' he said. 'When I first walked up to this place it appeared there was a need for a man's hand here and there.' He hadn't seen, he'd been too far gone. 'Fer one thing,' he added, 'I could move thet stove. Kinda makes it hot in here — encourages the flies.'

She stared at him, petulant. 'Why should I let you stay?'

He pursed his lips. 'No reason, I guess.' He raised dark brows. 'Jest thet Ma an' Pa used to talk a lot about common humanity — a need fer folk to help an' care fer each other, if they could, or if they needed it.'

She shuffled her feet, looked almost scornful of the words. 'They did?' Her laugh was bitter. 'Well, I seen little o' thet myself — lately, leastways.' Her stare was hard as it met his. 'I don't need any help around here right now. I don't want trouble. You understand what I'm talkin' about?'

'I understand,' he said. 'But *I* need help, ma'am.'

She looked startled by that. She began looking at him dubiously. He knew he wasn't the most presentable of prospects at this particular moment. In fact, he must look a real hardcase. Which, of course, he was. He couldn't deny it.

After long moments of what appeared to be reluctant consideration, she made efforts to smooth her sweat-lanky hair. She said, 'Well, there are a few chores need doin' around the place, I guess. But I ain't sure. Cousin tol' me to stay close, mind m' own

85

business, not be fussed with strangers. You got to be gone before he returns.'

'I'll be gone,' he said.

Again she looked at him. She began pacing over the buffalo pelts, while wafting the flies away. Then she stopped abruptly, stared directly at him. 'OK. Stew's about ready.' She pointed to his neatly mended clothing on the double tier bed opposite. 'I washed an' mended yuh duds, case you ain't noticed. I'd like you to bathe in the creek, too. When he was alive my Pa allus said a man should take some care of his appearance, no matter what his circumstances. To put it bluntly, you stink to high heaven an' need a shave, Wolf Strange.' She waved a finger. 'Cousin's spare razor is on thet shelf there. You kin git on with thet while I'm dishin' out.' Then she went to a shelf on the wall. She tossed crude soap on to the bed, looked at him and raised her brows.

He nodded soberly. In some ways her strictures reminded him of Ma. 'I'm beholden, ma'am. I promise, you won't regret your kindness.'

'I won't?' She thrust the clothes at him. 'Guess time will tell on thet.'

Wolf now sniffed. There was one other thing . . .

'There was a money belt. Considerable money in it. You got it?'

She gave him another direct, resentful stare. 'You think I stole it? It's under the bed. It ain't been touched, if thet's what you're thinkin'.'

He relaxed. By God, straight as a die, he thought. He said, 'No, ma'am, I wasn't fully. But I must confess, I had doubts.'

He left it there when he saw her hackles rising. *'Bathe yourself'*, she said. *'You stink.'*

It took some manoeuvring to hold the blanket to hide his nudity and to take the clothes and razor off her. She watched him. A twinkle came to her eye, a curl to her rosebud lips. When she spoke she did not hide her jeering tone. 'What you coverin' up fer? You figure I don't know all about you by now, Wolf Strange?'

Her mocking taunts brought heat to his drawn cheeks. 'Even so, ma'am, I figure there are certain decencies a man should observe in the presence of a lady.'

'Yuh do?' She raised her brows. 'Lordy me! Well, let's get one thing straight, mister, I ain't a *ma'am* yet, nor am I a lady, though I'm flattered. I'm nineteen years old, unmarried, an' the name's Jenny Braison. I'm tellin' you this because I already know who you are, Wolf Strange.'

Sassy as hell, too, he thought. Or was it a defence? He pulled the blanket and clothes to him, picked up the rifle. At the small door he paused and looked out. Not for the first time, a deep animal caution reared up in him, nurtured by dozens of gut-jerking skirmishes deep in enemy country and hackle-raising chases.

'When you turn, I'll see your ass, Wolfy,' she mocked.

He stared at her. *OK, Jenny Braison.* He said, 'Jest make sure you don't lick it when I do . . . *ma'am.*'

Outside he paused again and took in the whole basin area. Clear as far as he could see. On the western horizon, the low sun was sliced by thin clouds into stratas of red, gold and purple. To the east, mauve shadows were already developing. A few birds were giving out with sleepy chirps in the willows by the creek. A coyote yipped, far away. Cattle bawled and coughed downriver.

At the creek he laid his rifle on the bank, dropped the blanket off his stark white skin, brown only from the neck up and the wrists down and waded in. Three minutes later he splashed out, the milky water and suds left after his ablutions drifting downstream. The sun now daubed the mile-wide basin in blood-red light. Everything was red. Using touch he scraped off what beard he could, dressed, feeling refreshed but still grimly cautious.

When he arrived back at the dugout she had the meal laid out on the rough-hewn table. Two candles illuminated the dark interior. Their weak yellow light hardly killed the lurid red of the dying sun slanting in through the small door.

He was only mildly surprised when she insisted on pressing hands together and thanking God for his bounty before they ate. Only one thing marred the benediction: it took him back to blessed suppers at home and the terrible ache was renewed. He wondered if he ever would fully come to terms with his loss.

He was soaking up the broth in the bottom of the wooden bowl with dark, coarse bread when the first night bird chittered in the dark. Way out, as yet, but it was the kind of night warbler you'd hear on the Kansas-Missouri border, not — as far as he knew — on the Texas plains.

He should have known. He had thought it had been too easy this afternoon. Fenger never gave up that easily. The captain had just decided not to take chances, bide his time, assume the cholera claim to be legitimate until it was proved otherwise.

5

The woman paused in clearing away the supper things. She stared at Wolf with big, round eyes, as if she sensed his sudden concern.

'Somethin's wrong, ain't it?' she said.

Wolf strapped on his holster belt, cased one Colt Army in the holster, tucked the other with five loads in it in his belt, then picked up his Henry rifle. The brass on the long gun gleamed in the yellow candlelight.

'Get your rifle, ma'am,' he said. 'What clothes you have. Throw some food into a sack. I'll fill the canteens at the creek.'

Her face grew pale, though the interior of the dugout was stifling, but when her reply came it had a tone of petulance. 'Why?'

'I figure we still got company,' he said. 'They on'y half-believed your story this afternoon an' have waited. Guess I might have made a mistake, goin' down to the creek while it was still light.'

She stared at him. 'Why didn't they come straight down here when they saw you?'

'They got time to wait. They knew they'd take a lot of casualties if they tried to.' He made a sardonic grin. 'You'll recall I have a reputation. I figure they've decided to sneak up on us in the dark. They'd maybe have got away with it, too, if they hadn't set up their warblin' jest now.'

'But, they don't want *me*,' she said.

He looked at her. For all her occasional aggressive worldliness, it seemed she still had a quaint innocence regarding some things. 'You lied to them,' he said. 'You ought to know they wouldn't like that.'

She stared at him for a few moments. Clearly a battle was going on in her mind before she went for the Volcanic. She also grabbed a green dress hung on a peg driven into the earth wall. Then she picked up a hessian bag near the dead stove and went to a chest against the opposite wall, lifted the lid and took out flour, bacon, beans, a pan and two tin plates, some other things and stuffed them into the sack.

He immediately relieved her of their weight. 'We crawl out,' he said.

She nodded. Her face was now deathly pale, her eyes round and scared.

Excitement tingling in him, Wolf stared at the black oblong of night outside the open door. 'We head for the horses. You got spare saddles?'

'In the sod hut, down by the corral,' she said. 'What about the candles? We blow them out? They cost, you know.'

Jolted by her prudence at a time like this he said, 'You serious? They stay lit. Want 'em to think we're still in here.'

Not waiting for argument, he bellied across the buffalo pelts and through the low door. Outside, the bright stars gave some light, but not much. Tightening his nerve ends up further, more night calls chittered out in the basin and were answered.

'Lead on, Miss Braison,' he breathed.

'I'm called Jenny, damn it.' Her reply held a tinge of annoyance.

At the corral, the horses moved restlessly. Wolf padded past them to the small sod hut. Jenny moved silently behind him. He got out saddles and bridles. The rigs, he noticed, were well-used with renewed stitching to make them still serviceable. The girth-straps were worn but sound.

Back at the corral one of the horses, a piebald, went straight to Jenny, obviously hers. He settled for the big chestnut gelding rather than the small sorrel mare that was also in the corral. He turned the sorrel out to fend for itself. Then, with Jenny, he saddled up and mounted.

'This afternoon,' he said. 'Which way did they move out?'

'West.'

'So head north. We'll try an' get around them.'

Without comment she urged the piebald into the night and he eased in the gelding behind her. The chestnut had a fluid, easy gait. The ripple of its muscles under him suggested strength and stamina.

They'd hardly been in their saddles a minute when they blundered into a man standing in some brush, gripping the bridle on his horse, his head cocked, listening. He was maybe thirty yards away when they first spotted him; a dark bulk in the starlight. Obviously he'd heard them coming. Wolf's one thought was ferocious concerning their ill-luck. Damn it! They'd have to try and brass it out.

Still walking their mounts at a fast pace they were within a dozen yards of him, veering to avoid him, when he called, 'Who's thet?' Then he crouched, began pawing for the gun stuck in his waist belt. 'Oh, Jesus Christ. Strange!'

The star-shine gave Wolf enough light. His Henry rifle already in hand, he swung it up to his shoulder and fired as the Red Leg brought up his Colt and let loose. Wolf saw his hard face was a desperate mask behind the gun flash. Satisfaction came to Wolf as the man gave out with a harsh yell and staggered back. The Red Leg's own shot headed out into the night, way above Wolf's head. Jenny screamed, once.

Wolf yelled earnestly to her, 'Ride!'

She took off like a startled deer, batting her horse with the Volcanic rifle. Atop his own mount he kicked heels into the gelding's flanks, urging it after her.

All around, shouts began erupting out of the dark. The man on the ground was shouting, 'The bastard's over here, boys.'

Wolf fired again as he went past him. The man cried out hoarsely as the lead smacked into him. He flopped back on to the ground, moaning loudly and holding his chest.

Now Wolf heard guns begin to boom behind him, but there was no vicious hiss of lead passing to say their pursuers had located their mark. He urged the woman, 'Get us to some cover.'

'Shouldn't we be runnin' like hell away from here?' Her question bubbled with disbelief.

'Just do it!' he yelled.

Muttering, she swung her horse to the right. Soon Wolf found they were entering a large patch of willow and cottonwoods. In parts, the undergrowth growing with the timber was thick, affording good cover.

Hardly into it he said, 'Dismount. We'll try an' case them in a crossfire. Get them to hole-up out there.'

Momentarily she stared at him, big-eyed and white-faced, then swung down. He could see she was dubious about this manoeuvre. He felt instant anger. What the hell did she know? Sure, it wasn't in the manuals on hightailing it, but he'd learnt a man shouldn't do what he was expected to do. Ever.

With a stubby finger he indicated a place fifty yards up the creek. 'When you git in cover up there, wait for my shout, then make it hot for them with thet Volcanic. You hear me?'

Without reply she moved off. He took the horses and tethered them twenty-five yards back, then returned to his position. Moments later he heard the movement of horses ahead, closing in fast, too fast.

'Fire!' he yelled.

Almost before the order had passed his lips, the Volcanic began to boom. Hard on its heels Wolf brought the Henry into play. The cracks of their weapons began to punctuate the night.

Immediately ahead there were sounds of startled chaos, then Wolf recognized Fenger's command. 'We hold here. Dismount. Spread out!'

Wolf reckoned the captain's trash were about a hundred yards away. Lead began to clatter and racket through the trees around him.

Wolf reloaded, answered by aiming at the gun flashes. He sent off a volley of shots then quickly bellied to Jenny's position. Her big eyes met his hard stare. 'My gun's empty,' she said. 'Got no more ammunition. Cousin said these rimfire's weren't the most reliable of weapons anyway.'

'The man knows his guns,' Wolf said.

He pulled the Colt Army in his belt and handed it to her. 'You got five shots to play with, but don't use 'em yet. We git to the horses now. I figure they'll be filterin' in on us soon as they git over the shock. I reckon we've done enough to slow 'em down fer a spell, keep 'em guessin'.'

Her big eyes fixed on him. Clearly, she continued to be full of doubt. She hunched her slim shoulders nonchalantly. 'Seems a crazy way of doin' things, but you're runnin' the show, I guess.'

Resentful of her disapproval of his tactics he said, 'Jest don't fergit it. Can't do with a woman mouthin' off right now.'

Her stare flashed. 'I know the country. You don't.'

To release his anger Wolf leashed three shots into the night, then said, 'Git to the horses, lead out. An' be damned quiet about it.'

She rounded her eyes. 'Where to?'

'Back to the dugout, then west.'

'The *dugout*?'

'Yes, damn it. Figure it's the last place they'll think we'll light out fer.'

'You're doin' a lot of figurin',' she said.

'Jest git!' he hissed.

A flurry of gunfire rose up. As lead rattled around them, Wolf ducked instinctively, pulling Jenny down with him. He answered the gunflashes with more shots. Then he said, 'Know of any settlements around here?'

Though she clearly thought it was another fool question at this point she said, 'Benson's Crossing. Only one fer a hundred miles. South-west o' here. My cousin gits his supplies from there when he's around.'

Wolf nodded. 'If the dugout plan works out an' we git clear of them, we'll make fer it. Now, move to the horses. We'll lead them fer a while. Don't want any sound to let 'em know we're runnin'.'

They'd walked leading their mounts for little more than a minute when Wolf realized his scheme wasn't working. Behind, the pound of hooves again began to quarrel with the night and he cursed silently as gunfire started popping once more. Mounting, he urged the gelding into the starlit darkness. Jenny matched his agility. Above the hiss of the wind created by his anxious ride he called, 'Fergit the dugout. Moon'll be up pretty soon. Know another place we can hole up? A real good place?'

The wind snatched at her voice. 'Mallan's Butte. Ten miles north. But — '

He said, 'Head fer it. Maybe we can make a stand there if we don't lose 'em.'

She didn't argue and urged her mount on. They soon put distance between themselves and Fenger's troop. Then she eased up her piebald and stared at him. 'This is crazy. If they lose our trail tonight they'll pick it up in the mornin'. I got a better idea to shake 'em off . . . permanent. Follow me.'

Angered again, he yelled, 'Damn it! Forgit it. Jest get us to the rocks.'

'To hell with that,' she said. She urged her piebald into the night. Enraged, he sent the gelding after her. Damn the woman.

Riding hard and confidently she made a big, ranging loop for a mile or more before cutting in to take them near to the north rise of the basin. Then, before he could do anything, she pulled his Colt Army from the belt around the man's shabby coat she put on over her dress in the dugout and fired three shots into the night.

He cut in close and glared at her. 'What in damnation! You gone crazy? You're tellin' 'em right where we are!'

Her face, though still deathly white in the starlight, was calm. 'I want 'em to run straight on to us,' she said. 'You wanna know why?'

He was wrathful. 'You can bet your damned boots I do.'

'I jest took a detour around a prairie-dog town,' she said. 'When they git their hocks in them holes it won't be only the hosses thet are goin' to git tilted over an' knocked about.'

Wolf opened his mouth to answer her, but no words came. Though he was reluctant to admit it, it was a shrewd plan the woman had come up with. He held his breath, taut with expectancy and stared into the night. It wasn't long before he heard the screams of hurt horses and the hoarse shouts of injured and confused men.

'Benson's Crossin' now?' she said calmly, a little smugly, he thought. 'Thet's where you said you wanted to go, ain't it?'

He turned to her. In the starlight her face wore a small, triumphant grin. Resenting it he rocked peevishly in the saddle. 'OK,' he said. 'So you got lucky.

But when you figure to pull another stunt like thet, let me know. I'll do the decidin'.'

She cocked her head, matched his glare. 'Thet so? Well, I figured on savin' my own hide, mister. You jest happened to be along. Git my drift? Anyways, there wasn't time to have a powwow about it.'

He fought to calm himself. He waggled a dictatorial finger to indicate the direction ahead. 'Jest move out now, will you, ma'am?'

Once more she glowered at him, her eyes cat-like and resentful. She snapped, 'I told you: my name's Jenny.'

He gripped the lead edge of the McClellan saddle he was astride and rocked, his anger seething in him. Again, damn the woman! For the first time in his life he felt as though he was a nothing, that something had finally snapped within him and his judgement had gone all to hell. It could be that he had become a desert of anxiety. Tired, wasted — weary of the years of war and the responsibility that had been thrust upon him and had become so much a part of his life for so long. The danger, the death, the constant hunger he had endured with the men he had been elected by them to lead. Damn it, *he* should be dead, not them. But instead, he had buried them all. Could it be, in the final analysis, their deaths were all his fault? That he had led them badly? Why, just now, he felt this woman had exposed his shortcomings?

He realized he was shaking — with exhaustion? — and was being riven with self-doubt. He stared at her. He said, gruffly, 'Git us to Benson's Crossing, ma'am.'

Then he could be done with her. He shouldn't have gotten her into this, anyhow.

After a moment's hesitation, while she seemed to study him with a depth he found disturbing, she urged her piebald into the prairie night.

Fighting his self-recrimination and petulance and the urge to ride alone, he finally edged the chestnut in beside her and matched the piebald's gait. But he still found it hard to come to terms with the fact he had been exposed, and by a chit of a girl. Look at her. She rode so easily, so confidently. She seemed to think the chase was over. Well, he knew better. Fenger and those bastards behind him would, like relentless hounds, be on his trail again before they had time to spit, despite what had happened just now.

He tightened down on his pettiness. God, what was the matter with him? The woman had gone way out on a limb to help him. He hunkered down in the saddle and glanced at her. She made a small, lonely figure hunched into her threadbare coat. She stared intently ahead. She sat astride her little piebald as if moulded to it, her dress pulled up, her legs bare to the knees. Her high, laced boots looked incongruous. But, like himself, he guessed this woman had known little happiness of late. Maybe she had known some fighting, too?

An hour later the moon rose, full and beautiful in the big sky. Soon it was filling the night with silver light and good eyesight could pick up movement at quite a distance. He eased down on the pace, to give the chestnut a breather and to check his back-trail.

With a sigh, suggesting she may have been waiting for an easing in his relentless canter, Jenny eased down on the little piebald. He'd noticed the animal was showing signs of distress, but the gelding under him still had a run in it. Sweeping the horizon with a narrow gaze, as far as he could ascertain there was no sign of pursuit. Satisfied, he reckoned they'd gained enough time to ease down on the pace and allow Jenny's small, game horse to recover.

* * *

Four days later and Wolf feeling much more relaxed and perky, they hit

Benson's Crossing. He saw it was a small sprawl of adobe buildings by a broad stream, but the green country around soon faded out to range land once more. He saw a solid rope ferry was rigged across the river.

It seemed to Wolf the settlement was there chiefly to dispense liquor and trail victuals to anyone who had the money to pay for them. On the ride in Jenny explained Benson's Crossing consisted of a general goods store, a liquor store and a doss house, all owned by Neal Benson. He owned the ferry, too. She went on to say a small, federal army post was established to the north, about four miles away, and that she knew the camp commandant and his wife. Her cousin told her if she got lonely or scared any time she should head for there until he returned. But all along Wolf had been of the opinion her cousin must be some sort of a bastard to leave her out there alone in the first place. Why not leave her at the fort until he got back and have done with it? But, maybe she hadn't wanted that. He hadn't pursued the matter. For sure, judging from what he had seen and experienced of her he found he could easily agree with that reckoning. He'd discovered she had a tough, independent streak in her. There was a deal about Jenny Braison that a man could admire, as well as feel pleased about.

As they overlooked the settlement from a low knoll, she cocked her head, stared at him. He'd discovered, the way she did the movement, it could almost be construed as a challenge. 'What are you going to do now, Wolf Strange? Stay around? I reckon my cousin would take you on fer the drive if you asked him. He's allus said the more hands there was, the bigger the herd they'll have to take to Sedalia.'

Feeling his cynicism, he met her stare. 'Ain't you fergittin' who I am, Jenny? Who your cousin *was*? He was a Jayhawker. I'm a ex-Missouri Raider. I don't think the combination will mix.'

Her look was disdainful. 'Well, *he's*

put that behind him. He ain't a vindictive man. He won't ask questions. He's said a lot o' men did a lot o' things in thet war they'd no cause to be proud of, himself included.'

'An' a lotta men did things they could be real proud of, too,' Wolf said. 'I count myself in thet.'

But her suggestion tempted him and not just for the start it would give him. On the ride here Jenny had proved good company. She could be bubbly and vivacious, when her guard was down. And she seemed to like him. Maybe in time, with his troubles solved and with a cash stake to set himself up with a farm or something like that, they could make a life for themselves . . .

He stared at her hair. It shone like a raven's wing in the sun. She usually covered it with a wide-brimmed slouch hat but had just removed it to allow her to shake it out and let it fall free to her shoulders. He knew why it shone, too. On the way here, whenever they hit water, she took time out to wash and comb it while he watched, absorbed in this woman's thing to keep themselves clean and prettied up.

He snapped his mind shut. All this was just crazy thinking. He and Jenny could never be more than they were at this moment, he couldn't allow them to be. Even if he shook Fenger, there were still the men who had killed his Pa and Ma. Their faces were branded into his memory. There could be only one fate for them and that would come out of the muzzles of his guns . . . even if it took a lifetime to do it.

Answering her he said, 'No. Got to be movin' on.'

He found it hard to hold the intense look that came to her grey eyes. 'What if I asked you to stay; said I liked you enough fer thet?'

Jolted by her frankness he stared. 'You crazy? I'm on the run. I got nothin' to give.' He waved a careless hand to his rear. 'Those men back there, they won't give up.'

But her deep-digging gaze remained

on him — unflinching, even fanatical. 'I've *chosen* you,' she said. 'Right from when you keeled over back there at the dugout, I had you figured as the man fer me.'

He stared at her more intensely, even resentfully. A woman, making all the damned moves? 'Well, you git thet idea outa your head right now,' he said. 'You ain't thinkin' straight.'

To avoid her stare he gazed indignantly across the range.

'Will you look at me, Wolf Strange?' She made it almost an order. He turned. Her chin was set. 'I'm thinkin' as straight as I ever will,' she said. 'I've come to the opinion I've found my man an' thet's it.'

His annoyance grew. He jutted his chin. 'Will yuh drop it? If you don't you'll not only torture me, you'll torture yourself. We ain't never goin' to have a life, Jenny. Git thet through your head.'

She started to ease the piebald forward, towards the settlement but her stare was still riveted on him and adamant. 'Try to run out on me an' I'll follow you,' she said.

His rage spurting up again, he urgently kneed the gelding to pull alongside her. 'Of all the knotheaded . . . will you fergit it?' he said. 'I figure I've got a few hours, then I'll be on the run again. Meantime, I'm goin' to git you near thet army camp an' safety. If Fenger calls in at the army post, you say I forced you at gunpoint to do what you did. Git thet major friend o' yourn to side you. You savvy me?'

Her gaze challenged him, making it obvious she didn't like the idea. 'I won't be a burden. I brung you to here, didn't I? I got you outa thet little scrape back there. Maybe I c'n do it agin.'

His rage sprang up. 'I said no, damn it!' He rocked in the saddle. 'Now, do I have to drag you to thet fort, or are you goin' of your own accord? I gotta have your decision. Time's a'pressin'.'

Spots of bright colour flamed under her eyes. 'Wolf Strange! You can go to hell, you hear me? You're picked.'

She kicked her piebald into a run and sent it off across the range. 'I'll be seein' you, y'hear?'

Torn, he stared after her. He was *picked*? She was crazy. But suddenly, now she was gone, all seemed so empty around him. The vibrance of her, and, now, he had to admit, the joy and challenge of being with her was suddenly not there, gone like a snuffed out light. It was as though something had been switched off, some exciting presence. In his young life he'd never known anything like her. The warm peace of her. Her calmness and practicality. Was he to be forever damned to be hounded until death? Soon he would be back to fear, anxiety — constantly staring at his backtrail. Not living. Existing.

He stared after her. She was fading away from him, across the dry land and he couldn't do a damn thing about it.

For once in his life he decided he needed a drink.

6

Benson's bar was a gloomy, low-raftered, two-roomed adobe. It stank. Benson was a big, hairy, sweating man. He stank, too. His bar was two rough-hewn planks nailed atop of two barrels. Casks of booze were on a table behind him, against the stained wall. Wolf decided the place was about as crude as you could get.

'Whiskey,' he said.

'You got money?' Benson's voice rattled like a scraped washboard. His searching black eyes were slightly bulging. Flies buzzed about him constantly. He occasionally made an effort to strike at them with the wipe in his hand.

Wolf laid coin on the bar. 'You got food?'

Seeing the money, Benson's disposition immediately improved. 'Sure.' He

116

raised black eyebrows off fatty eyelids and stared at the beaded doorway, back of the drinking place. 'Rosa. *Comida.*' He returned his gaze. 'You want to take a table?' As he spoke Benson nodded in the general direction of a long rough table with the bench drawn to it; at a number of barrels with wooden tops nailed to them placed around the dim interior. Wolf now saw there were four other men in the room, around one of the barrels, drinking and playing cards. Two were Bluebellies. They had to be from the post, he decided. They gave him close scrutiny, particularly the Reb hat he wore. With his eyes not yet used to the dark interior, he could hardly distinguish their features but there were no bad moves and he saw no cause for concern.

Wolf chose a barrel table against the far wall, taking the bottle Benson had handed him. He was into his third drink when the comely Mexican woman waddled in and placed before him a bowl of stewed chopped meat

117

and beans, then bustled out again. The first spoonful told him it was spicy, hot — very hot, but good. It was the first real food he'd had in weeks, apart from Jenny's hash at the dugout.

When he'd finished the meal he poured another measure from the bottle and downed it. It was awful stuff. He went to the bar.

'I need trail vittles,' he said.

'My store's down the way,' Benson said. 'I can fix you up.'

Wolf nodded. 'Soon as you can.'

That brought a closer, more knowing scrutiny from Benson, but that was all. It was clear he was a man who didn't ask questions, but had his suspicions. For sure, there must be a number of doubtful travellers passing this way these days. It wouldn't pay Benson to be too interested.

Benson called to the bead curtain again. 'Rosa. Watch the bar.' Then he turned to him while stripping off his filthy apron. 'Follow me, mister.'

Back in the bright daylight, Wolf

squinted and adjusted his vision once more. He collected the gelding and followed Benson down the track that led to the ferry. It could be passed off as a short street.

He found the store was as seedy-looking and gloomy as the drinking place. The smells were different here, though, reminding him of other general stores he'd been in over the years.

'Bacon, beans, coffee, salt, oats for the horse,' he said. 'Tobacco. Slicker. Blanket. Enough food to last a healthy man a week.'

As the order was given, Benson didn't bat an eyelid. He gathered the requested items together then said, 'Figure I've seen that horse o' yourn someplace.'

Wolf's stare was quick and cold. 'It's paid fer.'

Benson's reply was swift, his smile disarming. 'Sure. Sure. Never figured otherwise.' He raised his bushy brows. 'You be usin' the ferry?'

'Reckon not.'

Benson put the supplies into a sack and stated the price. Wolf duly paid up and gathered them up, started for the door.

'Ferry's cheap,' said Benson moving to the door with him. 'Next ford is fifty miles north, 'less you're figurin' on swimming across. But I warn you, thet can be tricky. Quicksand, currents, snakes . . . real bad in places.'

Wolf eyed the trader. 'That so? Well, I'll find my own way. Ain't a mind to cross the river, yet. Figure to look around here awhile. Know of any work goin'?'

'Heard a fella name o' Goodnight is lookin' fer hands to take a herd to Fort Sumner, up New Mexico Territory. Gatherin' cattle west of here.' Benson tacked on, 'You'll need to git across the river fer that.'

Wolf secured the goods to the saddle and swung up. 'If I do you'll be seein' me agin,' he said then eased the chestnut up the track towards the open prairie. Benson locked up and followed on behind, ambling on short bowed legs.

As he rode, Wolf felt a calm urgency developing in him. For sure the Red Legs would be here shortly, so maybe would the army when Jenny Braison arrived at the post and recounted her story, though he wasn't sure about that. It would depend on how she told it. If he let Benson ferry him across the river, it would give his pursuers a lead as to the direction he lit out from here, for he was sure the trader would tell them without much pressure needing to be exerted, particularly if there was a buck in it.

Another thing he found intriguing: the talk about this fellow Goodnight gathering a herd to take to Fort Sumner. If he could join that it would give him an opportunity to lose himself for a year or so. Maybe by then the need to get him would have been toned down or, more hopefully, abandoned.

Fifty yards of steady jogging took him

abreast of Benson's drinking place. He noticed a small, round-faced man was now leaning against the adobe wall alongside the open door, arms folded. He faltered. There was something about him . . .

Wolf abruptly tensed, eased the chestnut to a stop and stared. Immediately, ice seemed to sprinkle a cold path down his backbone, sharding a prickling feeling through the rest of him. Those features . . . long ago seared into his brain. This was one of the men running from the brutal obscenity left at the homestead that terrible day when Pa and Ma had been slaughtered. There was no mistake.

He was smiling up at him. 'Saw you in the *cantina*, mister.' He squinted. 'Ain't I seen you before, someplace? The war, mebbe?'

Wolf assumed he had been one of the card players. Apart from the first perusal of their table he hadn't paid too much attention. He'd just wanted to eat, then get out.

'I reckon so,' he said.

The man grinned at him. It was tentative, half-friendly. He was a middle-aged man, busy-looking. A new single-action Colt was holstered low on his right hip. 'Back o' my mind I do seem to have a particular reason to know you.'

As he spoke Benson ambled up, took a stance in front of the adobe, glanced at each in turn. He was clearly anticipating something.

Wolf said, 'Does November '63 mean anythin'? Beely Creek Valley? The Strange place?'

The man came off the wall and moved into the sunlight. His blue gaze direct. 'Beely Creek? God, that was some time ago. We got certain orders, I remember. Sure, I was in some action around there.'

Wolf fought to keep calm. 'I'm Wolf Strange. I was the kid running along the trail after you'd fired my Pa's homestead. The man headin' you shot me. You left me fer dead.'

He watched the man tense, but the bastard tried to remain affable. 'Left you fer dead?' He grinned. 'You got me mixed up. Jesus, a lotta things were goin' on around thet time, a lotta hate was stirred up after the town o' Lawrence was burned, its men shot. Man, those killin's were done right in front o' their wives an' kids. A terrible thing. But, hell, I bin quit o' thet shit a year now. Pard, the war's over.'

Wolf said, 'It ain't fer me. Not yet. Things to tidy up.'

The man rubbed his chin stubble. 'Wolf Strange . . . I heard *somethin'* about you. Ain't they after you an' thet gang you ran with?' He grinned. 'Damn me, you're still around, huh? Well, good luck. Hope you make it. I got no malice.'

He's lying, Wolf thought. How could he stand there *grinning*, telling him he'd finished with his murdering ways, that he'd forgotten the terrible things he had done, wished him luck?

'What happened to the others you

were ridin' with thet day?' he said.

The man rubbed his chin again, looked puzzled. It was hard to tell he was faking it. 'Others?' he said. 'Hell, I was with two or three outfits. Allus movin' about, like you still are, I reckon. When the surrender came, I went my own way.' He squinted once more. 'Now, boy, what was thet about shootin' you on some damn trail or other? You tryin' to say I was in on those killin's you jest mentioned?'

Wolf caught movement at the open door of the drinking place. The two army boys who had been in on the card game drifted out of the adobe into the sunlight and joined Benson, leaning against the wall. Wolf quickly satisfied himself neither Bluebelly was carrying arms.

'Not on'y thet, mister,' he said, 'you burnt my Ma, gunned down my Pa — dragged him on the end of a rope until he was damn near pounded to a pulp, then tortured him before you cut off his cock and stuffed it in his mouth.'

Wolf leaned forward, his big frame full of menace, his eyes like flint arrowheads. '*Now do you recall*?'

The man blanched, began to shuffle in the dust, fidget with his ear, rub his right hand down his pants. He shook his head. 'Hell, I don't recall nothin' like thet, mister, nothin' at all.'

Wolf's stare turned steely. 'I think you're a liar.'

The man's gaze hardened. He licked his lips. His face became a stone mask, the — up until now — happy eyes the colour of fire-stained obsidian. 'No call fer thet,' he said. 'Like most, we had orders. All kinds o' orders.'

Wolf said, 'How about Order 11?'

The man cut air with a sweaty hand. 'Damn it, after Lawrence, it was called fer.' He wiped the perspiration from his upper lip. 'Hell, if there was resistance . . . ' He stopped, glared. 'Christ, you know as well as me things seldom worked out the way they was intended.'

'No, I don't,' Wolf said.

The man's fury was now clearly awakening, all affability gone. 'The hell you don't. You trying' to say Anderson, Quantrill, thet ilk, were lily-white, thet you didn't ride with thet kind of shit?'

'I'm sayin' my outfit fought as fair as it was allowed to.'

The man stared his disdain. 'Jesus, you're livin' in cuckooland.' He pointed a stubby finger. 'I've heard stories about thet outfit you rode with, boy, an' thet's why you got the Red Legs on your ass right now. Well, you ain't git a prayer, you hear me?'

Wolf smiled thinly. He said, 'I want names, mister. All the men you rode with that day. Now.'

The man sniggered. 'You do? Well, you can go to hell, boy!' With a lightning move, he stepped back, lips drawn back off his stained teeth, hand clawing for his Colt.

Wolf moved with him, yanking the big cap-and-ball Colt Army out of the belt over his coat. The bark of the two guns were in unison — harsh, yammering across the plain beyond the crossing.

Wolf felt lead burn heat across his face, but the man was teetering on legs that appeared to have turned to jelly. With a cry he buckled, flopped face down on the street. Blood from a hole in his chest crimsoned his grey vest and gaudy blue shirt and slowly spread into the dust.

Gasps came with movement to his left. Wolf swung around. He lengthened his arm and trained the Colt on Benson and the soldiers. The other card player staggered out of the door to stand blinking in the sun, mouth open, drink in his hand. One of the army men shot up his hands, 'Easy. We ain't armed, mister.'

Wolf nodded. He found a curious coldness was in him, a clinical abstraction. He'd never stood up, face to face, with the deliberate intention of killing a man before. The killings he had done had been in the heat of dozens of bloody skirmishes.

He flicked a glance at the body before he returned his gaze. 'Who was he?' he said.

The soldier doing the talking looked incredulous. 'You mean you don't know?'

Wolf glared. 'Would I be askin'?'

'Zack Boles we know him as.' The soldier gestured with a raised arm. 'Damn, he do what you said to your folks?'

'He'd still be alive if he hadn't.'

'A hell of a thing,' the soldier said. He narrowed his eyes, squinted. 'Wolf Strange, huh? Our outfit once tangled with yourn in the Ozarks.' He added, warmly, 'Mister, you gave us a real roastin'.'

Wolf gave him a cold stare. He found no soldier camaraderie in him. He'd come to think of such affability as being false, absurd.

'Thet so?' he said. 'Well, you won't git a cheer outa me.'

He pushed the warm Colt Army into

his belt, swung his chestnut and sent it towards the range.

Watching him go Benson relaxed, shook his round, greasy head. 'Now, there goes a man with a grudge,' he said. He stared at the soldiers. 'Boys, by God, after thet, I need a drink. You comin'? The first's on me.'

Both Bluebellies smiled and the newcomer who had most recently stepped out from the *cantina* swayed and also stretched a silly grin across his face and stared at them. He said, 'Now, how in the hell could we pass up an offer like thet, boys?'

One soldier offered a quick grin. 'Wouldn't be easy. So I'm follerin' you right in there, Horace.'

Meantime, unheeded, Zack Boles lay where he'd dropped. Only the flies were ministering to him in their own particular way. Maybe somebody would take the trouble to bury him later . . .

7

Jenny rode into the the army post tired. The camp commandant, Major John Bryant and his wife, Celia, came smiling out of their modest two-roomed adobe to meet her. It suggested they had been forewarned of her approach. A trooper was on hand to take her jaded piebald.

She knew the couple were in their early fifties and that they both strongly resented this posting. But now the war was over and officers and men were being stood down, they'd had to accept the situation — Major Bryant being a professional soldier for most of his life. Jenny knew her cousin had struck up a friendship with Major Bryant before the war in Kansas, which had continued ever since. Both men had strong views on the emancipation of the blacks.

Celia came forward immediately,

hugged her, then stepped back, delight in her gaze. 'Jenny, what a welcome surprise. You'll be stopping for a few days, of course.'

'If thet's all right.'

Celia made a mock scolding noise. She fussed with her green silk dress. 'Tch, tch. How you can stand living out there all alone when we're here?' Her eyes rounded. 'Why do you do it? It's no trouble to have you, child. We could soon build on a bedroom to accommodate you.' She smiled sweetly at her husband. 'John, you won't object to sleeping at Lieutenant Sobers' quarters during Jenny's stay?'

Tolerantly, if a little long-suffering, Major Bryant returned her smile. 'Do I ever have a choice, my dear?'

He stepped forward and Jenny accepted his gentle hands on her shoulders, his soft kiss on her forehead. Then he held her at arm's length. 'Now, what brings you to the post, Jenny?' He took in her shabby, dirty clothes. 'Trouble by the looks of it.'

Jenny tried to look dismissive. 'Oh, nothin' I wasn't able to handle.'

'I take it from that, you don't wish to tell us.' Major Bryant smiled again. 'But I'm sure Celia will coax it out of you before you leave us again.' He frowned. 'It wasn't Indians, was it?'

'No, it wasn't Indians.'

'Oh, leave her be, John,' scolded Celia Bryant. 'Come in, Jenny. You look worn out. I'm sure you could use a hot bath this instant. And I'm sure it won't be long before Lieutenant Sobers, and the other officers, will be here calling to pay their respects and you'll want to look your best. It isn't often we get a beautiful, eligible gal like you at this dreadful place to liven us all up.'

Though anticipated, Jenny accepted the invitation with a thankful sigh. And, yes, she was dirty and near exhausted. A bath would be luxurious bliss. She eagerly followed Celia into the major's quarters.

By suppertime she was bathed, rested and refreshed and changed into the fine silk dress her cousin had bought her in St Louis before they had moved out here. It was a prized possession and she kept it here for such visits. Now she sat with the Bryants, relishing the spread of food on their table. Buried out here as Celia was, Jenny always marvelled at how the major's wife managed such refinements to her cooking, her tasteful furnishing of their cramped quarters and how she managed to stay so cheerful.

She settled down to enjoy her meal, but she'd hardly begun when the sudden shouting and bustle of activity outside intruded on their light-hearted talk. Jenny tensed, listened intently. A squirm of anxiety riddled through her. She thought immediately of Wolf. God forbid. Had they caught him and killed him?

Wearing a frown Major Bryant rose, dabbed his mouth with his napkin as he listened to the commotion outside. He flicked a glance at his wife. 'Seems we have more company, my dear.'

He moved to the door and opened it. Jenny stayed seated with Celia Bryant, but through the open door, in the last of the orange twilight, she could see nine weary men walking their mounts into the post confines. Two horses were carrying double. Jenny saw it was Captain Fenger and his men.

After talk with the duty officer Fenger turned his tired horse towards the major's adobe. As he drew close, Major Bryant accepted his salute. Fenger looked dirty and haggard. At the major's request, he soon explained the reason for their arrival and their condition. One man had a broken collar bone, the other riding double had a broken femur. Then Captain Fenger explained the prairie-dog town incident. He went on to say, in the incident, one of his men had suffered a broken neck and three horses had had to be destroyed. When Fenger mentioned Wolf being behind it, Major Bryant perked up, then frowned and thoughtfully rubbed his resolute jaw. 'Hum.

135

That renegade. I remember him. A wily customer. I crossed his trail a couple of times in the Missouri border country. He and his men caused us endless trouble.'

Jenny saw Fenger was unimpressed by the information, or too weary to be. 'I have been given orders to hunt him down with all possible speed, Major. However, though we have decimated his gang we have yet to run *him* down. But I believe him to be the last of them. There is the possibility he now has a woman with him.'

Major Bryant leaned forward, again frowning. 'A *woman*?'

Fenger tiredly dismounted and stretched. 'Yes. We came upon this dugout — a very crude affair — maybe a hundred miles north-east of here. The woman was living there alone. When we questioned her, she claimed not to have seen Strange, but later events confirmed that, not only had she seen him, but was sheltering him.'

Once more Jenny felt a quibble of

nerves flutter across her stomach. She clamped her thin hands tight shut. She became aware that Celia Bryant's quick stare and questioning gaze had swung on to her.

'A dugout, you say?' Major Bryant said.

'Yes.' Fenger's stare was keen, direct. 'Do you know of it, sir?'

'I know of one.' Major Bryant turned his head. 'Jenny?'

Jenny felt Celia Bryant's hand gently press on her arm. When she met the major's wife's caring, violet look she saw it was troubled. 'Jenny . . . was it you? Where is the man they're talking about now? Do you know?'

Jenny found she couldn't answer Celia, found that guilt was causing her anguish. Already, in a way, she had deceived Celia and the major. Something she had never wanted to do. She just hadn't anticipated Fenger would come here, but when she thought about it where else would he go if he knew of the post's existence? She reluctantly moved to the door. Celia followed her.

As soon as Captain Fenger saw her, shock and amazement filled his drawn features. He pointed. 'By God, that's her.' His stare turned cold. The fading twilight filled his lean face full of hard shadows. 'I think you have some explaining to do, ma'am, and it had better be good.'

The jaded Red Legs also straightened when they saw her and scowled, some even edged hands towards weapons. Jenny felt her pulse begin to race once more. She was finding it difficult to form an answer.

'Well, Jenny,' Major Bryant said, 'is Captain Fenger correct?' His stare was puzzled, quizzical. 'We're waiting. What was your part in this affair.' He made a gentle, but nevertheless, the hint of an inquisitional gesture with his right hand. 'Did Strange molest you, force you into something? I cannot believe you acted voluntarily.'

Instantly, she felt compelled not to blacken Wolf if she could avoid it, although he had advised her to do so if such a situation as this arose. 'Oh, no. He didn't exactly force me. He — '

Captain Fenger cut in harshly, 'Then, what did he do? I warn you this is a serious matter, ma'am. Your answers had better be precise and plausible.'

Jenny found her brain was now working fast, but was also confused. She was still angry with Wolf. And, *why* did she feel this need to protect him? She had only known him a few days, fear-ridden ones at that, yet she wanted to defend him, cover for him even though he had *rejected* her, saying any relationship between them was impossible, which, rationally, it was, but she couldn't feel at all rational about Wolf Strange and that troubled her even more. She'd already told him how she felt and had meant it wholeheartedly.

She straightened and met Fenger's hard stare. 'When he came to the dugout he was very ill,' she said. 'I attended him. I jest did what most right thinkin' folks would have done. I had no way of knowin' who he was, or what he's supposed to have done.'

Fenger's face expressed irritation. 'You must have realized he was a renegade. A killer.'

Jenny raised her chin. 'No, I didn't. How could I? He didn't act like a killer. He acted gentle when he came to his senses. He was fevered fer three days.'

Captain Fenger 'humphed', lifted fiery ginger brows and turned to Major Bryant. 'Really, sir, are you listening to this?'

When the major turned to her, Jenny met his questioning stare. 'Jenny? Surely you can explain this business?'

'I've jest done so.' Agitated she waved her hand, shook her head. 'He passed out at my door. He was helpless. What could I do?'

Fenger interceded, 'Do? You lied to us, madam!' His blue eyes seemed to ignite with sudden anger. 'Where's your sick husband now?' A sneer smeared his face, as if he hadn't believed her story in the first place. 'Cholera, wasn't it?'

140

Before Jenny could answer, Celia Bryant gasped, 'Your *husband*, my dear? Cholera? What is Captain Fenger talking about?'

Jenny glanced at her, her mind racing. 'I was tired. I meant to tell you tonight, over supper.' She turned to Fenger. 'I invented the story of havin' a husband with cholera, in the hope you'd go away. Strange said he had nothing to lose, thet he would start shootin' at you if I didn't do as he asked an' got rid of you in some way.'

Fenger's laugh was harsh, dismissive, cynical. 'And you *believed* him? One man kill thirteen armed, alert militia? You can't be that naïve.'

Jenny stared, hotly. 'Yes. I believed it. I didn't want anybody killed. I did what I could to prevent any killin'.'

'A likely story,' Fenger said haughtily. 'Why, damn it, ma'am, you rode away with him; participated in his escape.' His stare became intense. 'When we gave chase, two began shooting at us. How do you account for that? Were you shooting? It certainly seems like it. You threatened us at the dugout with your rifle; claimed to be a dead shot with it.'

'He forced me to go with him.' Jenny waved her hands. She was unused to lying. Maybe she was naïve. She hadn't expected such an intensity of questioning under the major's protection. 'Another man joined us out on the range,' she said. 'It was they who were firing at you. They tied my hands, put a gag in my mouth. I couldn't even shout out to you or I would have done.'

'The prairie-dog town,' Fenger said. His fatigue now seemed to be dropping off him as the excitement of the interrogation gathered pace. 'They couldn't have known about that. You could.'

Jenny found nerves were now playing havoc with her as she sought answers. 'The other one knew,' she said. 'He must have hung around while Strange was sick at the dugout an' found it. He took us round it, then fired his gun to lead you across it.'

Jenny became aware, as they talked, that night had closed in. Through the open door the lit candles in silver candelabra at the centre of the dining-table cast yellow light on the haggard faces of the captain and the men under his command.

Fenger pointed a long finger. 'You are lying, madam,' he said. 'Plainly lying.' He glanced to Major Bryant. 'I think firmer measures are called for here, sir.' Jenny met his gaze as he swung angrily back to her. 'Where is Strange now, damn you, lady? I need to know quickly.'

Major Bryant stepped forward, his jaw jutting. 'Captain Fenger,' he said. 'I must protest. Jenny has obviously been badly frightened by her ordeal. Surely you can't imagine she is in cahoots with this renegade?'

Fenger tilted his chin. 'I know nothing, only what I have seen and experienced.' Once more Jenny met his bright stare. 'Where is Strange now?'

In her agitation she realized her

heart was pounding, drumming blood through her whole body like a mill race. She shook her head. 'I don't know. When we got near the post he let me go and rode off with his companion.'

Fenger's thin lips curled in a sneer. 'His companion? I know his men are all dead, madam! There was no other companion, as you keep insisting.'

Jenny's self-control broke and her temper flared up. 'Why don't you leave him in peace? He told me he'd only fought for what he believed in, like every other man.' She tilted her chin defiantly. 'An' how do you know all his men are dead?'

'Ha! So there is sympathy.' A fresh sneer smeared Fenger's sallow features. 'I know because two prisoners from his gang of cut-throats, before they were hanged for their crimes, told us.' Cold anger flashed in Fenger's eyes. 'Now, madam, I want this business over with. I have reports to make and a family law practice to return home to. This whole business has gone on far too long. Out with it!'

Major Bryant said, 'Really, sir, this is not the conduct of a Union officer. I must order you to desist. I can fully vouch for this young lady's good character. Her cousin nobly served our cause for quite some years. I am sure she has told you the truth and knows no more. As to her initial reaction to Strange's plight, it was what any caring gentlewoman would have done under the same circumstances. As to the rest of it: she was obviously forced into whatever she did.'

Fenger raised ginger brows, sighed and looked with tired indulgence at the major. 'Sir, I am obliged to be aggressive in my questioning. It is incumbent upon me to put an end to Strange. This lady may have vital information we could use. It is clear she is in sympathy with him, despite his alleged treatment of her.'

'Well, I cannot allow it to go on,' Bryant said, but he turned to Jenny, his erect demeanour appealing to her.

'*Have* you any more to add, Jenny? Something you think may help Captain Fenger? It is important you try to remember.'

Again, regretting she had to lie to the Bryants, Jenny shook her head. 'Nothing, Major. I'm sorry.'

She felt Celia's hand on her arm. 'Child, why didn't you tell us about this as soon as you arrived?' She frowned and shook her head, clearly unhappy. 'Tush. I knew there was something amiss as soon as I saw you. I could sense it.'

Jenny took out her handkerchief. She wanted to cry — for Celia. 'I hadn't been abused by Strange. I jest wanted to get the whole thing out of my mind. I jest didn't want to cause you worry.'

'All the same, my dear,' said Major Bryant, 'you should have mentioned it. We could have got after the scoundrel. The hours we have lost now could aid his complete escape. It is unfortunate, very unfortunate.'

Fenger said drily, 'Unfortunate indeed.'

He swivelled his gaze. Jenny met his cold stare once more. 'Now, ma'am, I want you to think hard. Did he let something slip while talking to this . . . er . . . companion of his? Where he was planning to go? Mexico, perhaps? Did he mention that?'

Distracting everyone, noise on the camp perimeter caused all eyes to turn. Neal Benson came rumbling into the post confines, urging, with slaps of the reins, a bony roan towing a flat wagon. Two soldiers were on the seat each side of him. Benson came to a stop before the major's quarters. He smiled drunkenly. He got to talking right away. 'Been a killin' at the crossin', Major. A man name o' Wolf Strange blowed away a fella named Zack Boles.'

Jenny's stomach nerves jumped once more. She put a hand on her breast and breathed in sharply.

Captain Fenger stared at Major Bryant triumphantly. 'Are you convinced now, sir? There you have it; an out-and-out killer.' He turned to

Benson. 'How long ago, man? Was another person with him?'

Benson's gaze was bleary. He squinted as he strove to pierce the gloom. 'Weren't no other man as I know of. Shootout happened mebbe an hour . . . two hours ago. Strange wus on his own.'

Fenger straightened, his features exultant. 'On his own.' He turned. 'Madam? What excuse have you now?'

Jenny felt let down by Wolf; first for killing somebody, then forcing her to lie some more. 'Mebbe he left Strange,' she said. 'How should I know?' She looked up at Benson. 'Why did he kill that man?'

The ferry owner stared, blinking watery eyes. 'Why, ma'am? Hell, because Zack Boles was out to kill him.'

Fenger snorted contemptuously. 'Does it matter why? Once again Strange reveals what he is. A savage. A danger to everybody.' He turned to John Bryant, an invigorated man. 'Major, I need fresh horses, victuals. This man

148

must be hunted down.'

Jenny said, 'But he isn't a killer. Desperate, yes, but not a killer.' She stared at Benson. 'Was there an argument?'

Benson focused his whiskey-blurred gaze. 'We got some drift. There'd been somethin' in the war — somethin' about Boles bein' part of the gang thet murdered Strange's folks. Both men drew 'bout the same time. Weren't nothin' unfair. Seemed to be jest a load a hate between them thet had to be got out.'

One of the soldiers beside him drunkenly nodded his agreement. 'Seemed thet way to me, too,' he said. He hiccupped.

Fenger growled with disgust. Seemingly tired of word fencing, or thought Jenny was an irrelevance now this new information had come in, he turned to Major Bryant. 'As I say, I need to get after him, sir. He can't have gotten far. His horse must be tired. Can you meet my requirements as soon as possible?'

Suddenly, Bryant was pure army. He nodded briskly. 'Of course. But first dine with us, Captain Fenger, while these matters are attended to. Some of your men clearly need medical treatment; those that don't could do with cleaning up and refreshment. By the way, I have a fine Indian tracker on the post. I will put him at your disposal.'

Fenger nodded aquiescence. 'My thanks, Major. I must agree, we could all do with a little respite.' He turned to his jaded Red Legs. 'Two hours, men. No more. We could have this matter done within a couple of days, then we will be able to return to our families.' He turned to Benson. 'Which way did the scoundrel go?'

Benson hiccupped. 'Asked him if he'd be usin' the ferry, but he headed out north. Said he wus lookin' fer work. His hoss weren't too good. Needed rest.'

The news filled Jenny with renewed anxiety. She could hardly contain her silence. She wanted to shout it was all

150

so unfair and for them to stop it. She balled her hands into fists. Her heart cried out. Oh, Wolf. Ride. Ride. But, again, she didn't know why she felt like this. Wolf Strange wasn't what Aunt Maud — when she was alive that is — would have called a 'catch' and she should forget him.

Fenger said, 'One more thing, Major.' His stare was hard. Jenny met it when it turned to settle on her. 'I would like the lady kept under supervision until this is over. I am not entirely satisfied she is what she claims.'

Clearly unhappy about the captain's distrust, Major Bryant paddled ground on shiny boots. 'Damn it, man, I won't have it.'

Standing by Jenny's side, Celia gasped, 'Yes, really, Captain Fenger, this is inexcusable. Jenny has been the victim of a most harrowing and dangerous event.'

Fenger stared at her keenly, then he sighed wearily, 'Very well, ma'am, I will put it another way.' He returned his stare to the major. 'Sir, may I request you entertain the lady as your guest — just for a week or so, but do not allow her to leave the camp. I make the suggestion merely as security for her. If she has been treated as she claims, surely the lady will welcome the chance to recover fully — feeling reassured by your protection and having the anxiety that Strange may return taken from her.'

Jenny met Major Bryant's beaming smile. 'There, Jenny,' he said. 'Don't you think that to be a very reasonable compromise? Captain Fenger clearly has your best interests at heart.'

Celia was also smiling happily. She said in her silvery voice, 'Yes. Oh, yes, indeed.' Jenny met her joyful violet gaze. 'Jenny, my dear, you must agree. You must be so shaken by your experiences. Let us help you to forget this horrible man.'

'Horrible?' Resentment welled up in Jenny.

Celia's eyes rounded, as if in

surprise. 'Why, yes. You can't believe he isn't, after the ordeal he has put you through?'

Jenny felt trapped, but decided she couldn't embarrass her friends any longer. They had done their best for her, as they saw it. As for Wolf being horrible . . . she'd avoid further comment on that.

'Well, I do feel very tired,' she said.

Beaming, Celia turned, her hands clasped together as if in prayer. 'So, that's settled, my dear.' She turned. 'Captain Fenger, come, freshen yourself up and eat with us while you are re-equipped.'

Fenger bowed stiffly. 'Gracious, ma'am, and gratefully accepted.' He stared sourly at Jenny as he went past her into the major's quarters.

8

Four miles north of Benson's Crossing, Wolf gazed across the river. Benson said snakes, currents and quicksands bedevilled these waters. Considering the risk, he pursed his lips. The broad stream looked peaceful enough. But the thing that was intriguing him most was the man Benson mentioned — Goodnight — who, he said, was taking a herd of cattle to Fort Sumner, New Mexico Territory. Wolf's stare became thoughtful. If he could link up with him . . .

He worked his wide shoulders. Every muscle and bone ached. He felt weakened and worn down by the merciless hunt he had been subjected to for so long. And he knew such listlessness, if he didn't shake out of it, would, at some time, mar his judgement, prompt him into actions he may well not find a way out of. If he was brutally honest, Jenny had saved his bacon back at the dugout.

He stared at the brush on the bank opposite. One more effort, get across the river then ride. Fenger would find his tracks, sure enough — he had succeeded in doing so up to now — but now he was a man alone perhaps he could mask his trail enough to lose himself in this vast land and lose Fenger, too.

He lifted out his Colts, tied rawhide around the trigger guards and hung them around his neck. At all times, he needed dry powder.

Feeling ready he stared at the dark, riffling waters once more, then took a deep breath and urged the horse into it. Gratifying him the chestnut began powerfully plunging through the chest high water, while all the time the current drifted them steadily downstream. Wolf held his rifle above his campaign hat and gave the horse its head. It soon became clear the gelding had a high instinct for survival. It

155

breasted through the water strongly and eagerly, its ears erect and alert.

Wolf watched the opposite bank draw progressively nearer. They were nearly there when the horse let out a squeal, began whiting its eyes, staring around at the swirling water. It was then Wolf saw the snakes; three, four of them swimming close. Immediate, desperate anxiety wrenched at his gut. One snake, too near, struck at his boot, but didn't penetrate the leather. With an angry cry, he kicked it away. Meanwhile, the gelding lunged strongly for the bank, its fright galvanizing it. Moments later, it clambered out and stood shivering, snorting and nodding its head in an agitated way. Wolf patted it, tried to calm it. But he could only allow it a few moments rest. He *had* to make ground. He couldn't spare the horse, or himself, even for a second. Setting his chin, he geed it out of the thin brush and struck out across the prairie.

As the gelding maintained a loping run, Wolf's confidence began to grow.

He was going to make it. Then, inexplicably, after only fifteen minutes from leaving the river, the horse began flagging, slowing down to a walk and occasionally tottering, despite his urging, anxious boot heels in its flanks. After a few more paces, it stopped, shuddered, then collapsed.

The sudden flop forced Wolf to jump to avoid the possibility of being rolled. However, the gelding, though down, still remained game. It tried to regain its feet but flopped back on to its side and began slobbering and snorting, its mouth open and slack. Frothy saliva began bubbling around its wobbling lips. All the time it struggled its eyes were flickering, as if in agitation. Now clearly delirious and still on its side, it began to attempt to run, its hooves scraping along the ground. It was as if its big heart was pathetically attempting to keep going for him, but all the gelding was doing was lying there scraping the hardpan and going nowhere.

In desperation, Wolf tried to get it up; pulling at the reins, cursing it. He *had* to get it up. But any damned fool could work out one of the snakes had bitten it and the run from the river had accelerated the poison's spread. The horse was slowly dying and he couldn't do a thing about it.

With a heavy heart, he stared at the struggling animal. There was only one thing left to any decent man to do and that was to save the beast further distress. He pulled out the Colt Army from his belt and stared down at the suffering gelding. At the last moment he stayed his trigger finger as another awesome possibility loomed. Damn it, if he did fire the weapon there would be big noise. He didn't know where Fenger and his dogs were. They could be thirty miles away, or they could be right up his ass. He couldn't take the chance shooting the beast posed.

He replaced the Colt and drew his long, honed battle knife. Over recent times he had acquired the ability to be able to kill *anything*, quickly and almost painlessly. Hating the need to do so in this case, nevertheless, he drove himself to the task . . .

★　★　★

After walking all night he halted in a hollow in some low hills, dug a hole and risked a fire. He cooked bacon, beans, brewed some coffee and ate with the relish of a hungry man. The meal over and feeling renewed, a glance to the east told him it was near to dawn. The first hints of pink and white-blue light, streaked with red clouds, were livening up the eastern horizon, slowly killing off the last of the stars. He welcomed it. Towards morning it had become real cool.

By the time he was on his fourth cup of coffee, in between clearing up the breakfast things, the darting shards from a golden sun, peeping above the immense horizon of the mauve prairie, unveiled the country around him:

grassland, reaching seemingly to infinity by the time it met the big sky.

With this full light, he could see the silver flicker of the river he had crossed in the far distance. He must have covered maybe twenty miles after he'd despatched the horse. He raised dark brows. Though not the ideal in a vast country like this, there was one thing about being afoot: a single man's tracks, as opposed to a horse's, would be even more difficult to find, if a man was careful about where he put his feet. And he'd been careful; careful as hell.

And, as was part of his nature now, to further spit in the eye of his situation, he felt real good about one thing — running into Zack Boles like he had. That was one hell of a lucky break. The encounter gave him a feeling of malevolent pleasure to know that one participant in the butchery and mutilation of his parents had met a just end.

He stared out across the prairie. So, it was one down, four to go. The only thing that marred the deadly meeting with Boles; he hadn't got names. Apart from Mitch Layton he only had faces to go on. However, that aside, if it took 'til hell froze over, he'd get the rest of those murdering killers. It was a sworn vow.

Drinking up the last dregs of his coffee he stared over his cup, once more towards the sparkling ribbon of river he had crossed and immediately his hand closed tightly around the enamel — an automatic gesture, filled with frustration and despairing anger. Faint dust was rising up into the gold light of the just-risen sun. Almost for sure a bunch of riders. It looked as though they'd not been long out of the water, maybe nearing where the horse lay. It had to be Fenger and his damnable Red Legs. An alien feeling of utter dejection began to press like a great weight on to his shoulders. The Devil roast the sonsofbitches! Would they never give up?

From this deliberately chosen high point he looked anxiously across the rounded backs of the rolling hills around him, fully revealed by bright daylight that was now filled with fluting lark song, though he hardly heard it. Three or four miles to the west he saw the hills there melded into an odd rampart of rock. The north and south sides formed steep escarpments. The rugged, immense mound stretched for at least eight miles into the vast distance before melding into the range. If he made that hunk of rock he would definitely leave no tracks and give himself more than an even chance to get out of this. Fenger and his rabble would have difficulty picking out the trail he'd already left, but along that bare, broken plateau it would become almost impossible. But, afoot like he was, would he make it in time? Or was he just too tired to bother any more?

He killed what was left of the fire, scraped earth over it, made it look as though nothing had been there, then gathered up his canteen and the remainder of his cooking utensils and food. That's all he had taken off the dead gelding — the worn saddle got off

Jenny Braison and the rest of his gear he had left. He had to travel light and hope he would come across a holding or settlement of some sort where he could buy a horse. He still had money to spend — Federal money.

Well before noon he gained the rampart of rock. But all morning the sun battered him, driving out what remaining energy his already-weakened body had, causing him to occasionally totter and drink more freely than he should from his canteen. Then, as if by some miracle, he very nearly fell into a tank of water that just appeared in the broken caprock. It seemed a complete incongruity in this semi-dry area. Everything said it shouldn't be there. But there it was, perhaps welling up through the rock formation from somewhere deep down in the earth's bowels. He stared covetously at it. What did it matter where it came from? It could help save him. He tested it — brackish but drinkable. He filled his canteen, sloshed his head, face, body, laid aside his weapons, then dropped into the pool and wallowed luxuriously.

Ten minutes later he climbed out invigorated, new will to keep fighting welling up in him. Almost with contempt, he stared at his back trail. He must be shaking them. But, like a toppled house of cards, his joy sank. Still there and closer — the train of dust, moving slowly, inexorably towards him. He felt an urge to cry, but knew it was only his desperate exhaustion that was weakening his resolve. Anger soon replaced it. He glared with fierce eyes. Damn them all! Couldn't they give a man a break? And, in particular, damn Fenger. Near a thousand miles the bastard had trailed him. He figured the others would have given up long ago had it not been for him.

He gathered up his guns, food sack, replaced his battered Confederate hat. Since joining the guerrillas he'd worn it proudly, like battle flag. The jaunty tilt he gave to it announced his defiance, too. Again he stared at the seemingly unswervable progression of the dust cloud, belligerent challenge welling up. He envisaged the relentless captain. This is who I am, Fenger, he thought. I'm not ashamed of what I've done. Come an get me if you can.

He began walking again. Within minutes his wringing wet clothes were dry once more and his own sweat began to soak them again. And to add to his discomfort, a hot, burning breeze sprang up and began hissing through the stratas of serried rock stepping up each side of him. With it, buzzards began lifting on the air currents — spiralling higher and higher until they were specks in the sky. A coldness hit his stomach for a moment. Surely, they weren't looking for him?

Mid-afternoon he paused again, climbed a heap of rock and looked back. The dust cloud had now stopped at the beginnings of the rock mass. Clearly there was indecision within the party. Yes, they had been slowed down, presumably been forced to search hard for his tracks. As he watched they started off at an angle into the prairie again. Seeing their confusion, cautious elation welled up in him. Maybe his plan was working.

Strengthened by their apparent chagrin, he sat down under the shade of an overhang, took a draught of water. For reassurance, he watched the Red Leg troop for more minutes, then felt his gut clamp up once more when they halted again. More doubt appeared to have arisen amongst them. After what seemed a short debate they split up, one bunch going back to a point that would bring them up on to the top of the rock formation, the other group heading off down the south side of the escarpment to where the long bulk of rock melted down into the undulating grasslands once more.

A flinty look came to Wolf's gaze. It didn't take a genius to work out they were going to try and box him.

Once more desperation rose up. His brain began to race, scratching in the fatigue-dulled corners of his mind for answers. He stared around him, grim-faced, his gaze ranging over the weathered caprock. He had two options: the first one, and the most extreme, was to find a good, defendable area and shoot it out to a finish. Option two, keep moving and try to out-think them. Damn, if only he could reason straight, shake off this tiredness. A week's rest at Jenny Braison's would have made a new man of him.

With grey eyes he considered the north edge of this rocky aberration he was traversing. It was maybe half a mile away. It was the side Fenger hadn't bothered to cover. Perhaps he'd looked at it and considered it too precipitous? From where he was it must have seemed to drop off too steeply, like the south side did. Maybe it did?

Twenty minutes of arduous, strength-draining travel across the uneven plateau Wolf found that to be true. It plummeted 250 feet, almost sheer, to the prairie floor. Damn it, he never had been a rock-scaling man.

He wiped sweat from his brow. No wonder Fenger hadn't bothered to cover it. Grimly, he stared down the almost smooth face, searching for a likely route. It took some time, then, yes . . . a little further along the rim of the escarpment. Clearly, with his limited ability it wouldn't be an easy descent, but the best available by the looks of it.

He split a hole in his food sack, hoisted it as best he could to his shoulder to allow him the use of two hands. It was cumbersome, unbalancing, but it was his means of sustenance — a chance of survival and it had to go with him. So far he had seen nothing out there that would suggest a settlement or a ranch where he could get food and a horse.

He wiped more sweat from his brow. He knew it was not only perspiration caused by the incessant heat, there was apprehension causing it as well. Subduing it, he started edging down. He immediately found the rock face, like the plateau, was burning hot, scorching his feet through the worn-out soles of his boots and searing his hands. He gritted his teeth against it as he gripped the stone. He soon found the footings he gained were crumbly and needing the greatest of concentration to negotiate.

He was maybe halfway down when a toehold collapsed under him, wrenching from him a despairing cry as he only had time to grasp desperately at a knob of rock with one hand before he was to begin plummeting down.

As the clatter of falling stone faded below him, he found himself hanging there, the silence, except for his rasping breathing, unbearable — the crushing, desolate feeling of defeat and despair veined right through him.

His body quivering, he dug deep into his reserves of guts and strength, reserves he thought were played out. He gingerly began searching for a toehold. He couldn't find one. The weight of his body, the weight of the sack of food, the weight of his rifle slung across his shoulders and the weight of his Colts in holster and belt began to pull on his arm, creating terrible strain. It seemed as if their combined weight was threatening to wrench the arm he clung to the face with out of its socket.

He had to get the pressure off his hand, his arm. Already his fingers were becoming numb, losing feeling, beginning to slip. He lunged up with the arm holding his sack of food, grasping for another handhold he spotted. He failed. The pans in the sack clattered against the rock. He blinked sweat out of his eyes. Only one thing left to do — let it go and salvage what was left when he got to the bottom.

He allowed the food sack to slide off his shoulder. It clattered down until it hit the base of the escarpment with a crash of metal, then came the awesome silence again, once more broken only by his own harsh breathing.

Again, he lunged up. This time he

grasped the hand hold, secured his grip on it, then he anxiously searched with his feet. Soon, his sense of touch discerned a slender ledge beneath his right foot. Blessed easement came to his arms as he quickly found another toehold and rested, his breath sobbing harshly out of him.

Then, out of habit, before starting down again he glanced east, across the harsh land. The shock at what he saw caused his already thumping heart to beat like a racing trip hammer. He saw dust again, around a mile away. This time he reckoned it was a single rider. Whatever. One thing was for sure, he had to get off the rock face; if he didn't, it would be like a turkey shoot and he would be the turkey.

The rest of the descent proved comparatively easy. The lower he got, the kinder the slope of the rock. Once more on solid ground he stared at his trembling hands and feet. They were raw and bleeding. He flopped down at the base of the escarpment and rested, taking a long draught of water from his canteen while commencing to search the grasslands for the rider again. It had to be one of Fenger's men. It would be out of character for Fenger not to cover all the options.

For the first time in his life Wolf felt real, utter, abject defeat, the feeling he had reached the last showdown.

★ ★ ★

After studying the huge, fearsome bulwark of rock ahead, Captain Fenger decided on a probe into the prairie first. The strategy was reasonable. Strange was afoot. In a land as vast as this, that was almost a death sentence in itself. The renegade couldn't have got far. Fenger lifted his ginger-stubbled chin. That fact gave him time to pursue his options methodically. First, he gave the order to move south.

After half an hour, he ordered a stop and mopped his brow. Seated on his pinto beside him was Little Talk, the tall, fierce-looking Comanche guide Major Bryant had allocated to him. During their progress across the prairie the Indian had been constantly searching the ground for tracks. Little Talk, he discovered early on, had a tortured English vocabulary. By his sullen looks Fenger now decided the Indian was making it clear he did not agree with this tentative probe across the grasslands. Finally the arrogant native broke his silence.

'Him not go this way.'

Fenger stared at him. As leader of the troop he had to impress all of that sure fact that he was *leader*. As his father had always said, some men were born to lead, others to follow. He, he had been assured, was born to lead.

'Move ahead,' he said firmly. 'Continue to look for tracks.'

Little Talk's look was scornful. He shook his head. 'Crazy man. But you soldier chief, I guess.'

With kicks from his moccasin-clad heels, the Comanche urged his pinto ahead, his eagle gaze searching the ground. Fenger stared broodingly after him.

After half an hour of slowly following the Indian, Fenger began to think that Little Talk's abrupt opinion was right. He watched as the Comanche turned back towards them again. From leaving the Benson's Crossing army post, Little Talk had demonstrated remarkable tracking powers by bringing them swiftly and unerringly to Strange's early morning camp. And now, though he felt it might impair his authority and expose his judgement a little, he felt he should bow to Little Talk's superior abilities and hear what the stinking scoundrel had to say about the situation. Fenger allowed himself a small, ironic smile. It did please him to occasionally flex his command muscles, though, just for the hell of it.

As he drew close, Little Talk said, 'Him make no tracks here.' He pointed a brown finger at the huge mound of rock. 'Like say before, him take off up

174

there.' Once again a sneer enlarged the wide gash that was the Indian's mouth. His look expressed his contempt for the man they were tracking. 'Him think he fool Little Talk.' He continued to point his digit, but at himself this time. 'This Indian not fooled.' He nodded at the towering rock formation. 'Him fooled.' Little Talk burst out a harsh laugh.

Though finding Little Talk's arrogance unpalatable, Fenger nodded his agreement. A cold satisfaction filled him. After all this time Strange had finally backed himself into a corner. With his horse dead and set afoot in this vast, dry country, it appeared Strange was attempting to have his last desperate fling. Fenger arched his ginger brows. One had to admire the man. He had proved to be a tenacious, ferocious survivor.

Fenger smiled. Relishing his boast of yesterday — that he would have the matter of Strange done with in two days' time so he could turn for home — he felt superior. He would send half his men on to the rugged plateau, the other half down the south side of the escarpment to wait for Strange's emergence at the other end. Box the renegade in other words. The sides of the plateau were clearly too steep to be descended by a man without the necessary equipment. Strange certainly hadn't got that. Yes, the man was trapped.

He felt obliged to explain the scheme to Little Talk. He decided he would pay lip-service to the Indian's primitive instincts and to appear grateful for Major Bryant's assistance in loaning the Indian to him. But, to his chagrin, the Comanche looked only half-impressed with his scheme. 'Not good plan,' he said haughtily.

For the first time Fenger stared coldly. Expert though the savage was at the job he was brought along to do, the captain heartily resented the savage's assumption he had a better knowledge of strategy.

He said, 'Explain.'

Little Talk said, 'Rock has other side, too, huh? So, Little Talk take a look that side. OK? Him maybe climb down.'

Fenger felt contempt. 'It's too steep. I know the man we chase wouldn't be fool enough to attempt that.'

Little Talk gazed, his hawk features and black eyes impassive. 'Still take look. You, soldier chief, have plenty men to look other places. Not need Little Talk right now. He take look other side. Son of bitch maybe fool you, but not Little Talk.'

Irritated though he was by Little Talk's arrogance, Fenger nodded. After all, on second thoughts, Strange could be fool enough. 'Very well.' On an impulse, he said, 'You may take my spare long glass, too.' He dug the small telescope out of his saddle-bag — he'd taken it off a dead Confederate, anyway — and offered it to the Indian. 'If you do see him making the descent, keep your distance and report back to me at once.'

The tall, powerful Comanche in his

stained army tunic, bullet bandoleer across his deep chest, deerskin covering his loins and crotch and beaded moccasins on his feet, grinned, took the telescope and waved it, clearly immensely pleased to be given the honour of using it. 'Know how use long glass. No need report back. When Little Talk see man, fix him, real good.' He looked around him with slight contempt. 'No need for white men. Little Talk big warrior. He take care of it.'

Fenger sucked in impatient air. With a long finger he indicated around to his tired, dusty men. 'That pleasure will be ours, Little Talk.' With steel-blue gaze he glanced vaguely to the east and pointed his finger there. 'We have come a long, long way for this moment. You will report to me first. You understand? Those are my orders. *That man is ours.*'

Little Talk grinned. 'If man fight, Little Talk fight. *Waugh*!' He sent his horse lunging off over the brown grass toward the north escarpment.

★　★　★

Wolf gathered up what he could salvage from his spilled food and cooking utensils. All the time he watched the solitary dust trail edging its way in his direction. As far as he could discern, it *was* one rider. A cold, steely light came to Wolf's bitter gaze. Well, now, with a horse a man could do a lot of things he couldn't without one. Like get shuck of Fenger and his men, for instance. He continued to stare at the rider. And, it appeared, that bastard intended coming after him.

He ducked down, left his food sack, took off into the tall, already browning grass. A hundred yards out and satisfied with the position he found he settled and watched the rider come ever nearer. At 300 yards the horseman paused, studied the area Wolf had just vacated, then looked around, like an uncertain predator. Wolf saw he had a single feather in his braided hair. *An Indian*, by God. He had to be a scout from the post Jenny talked about, because of the shiny buttons on his Bluebelly tunic. Wolf stared around him, looking for better cover, but found none. He had already chosen well. He returned his gaze and was immediately startled to skin-prickling tenseness. The Indian had disappeared, only the pinto horse was standing there, cropping the grass.

Hardening his gaze and shallowing his breathing Wolf held tight, looked for any slight movement of the tall, hissing grass. The birdsong had now stopped. A deadly silence reigned on the prairie, where, moments ago, it seemed to be teeming with life. He took a fresh grip on the Henry rifle. He would have preferred to use the knife, but, in a situation like this, any method would do. For sure, he had to have that horse.

The grass he crouched in was hot, the insects a constant buzz around him. They were crawling over him, irritating him, but he couldn't allow them to distract him. He heard a dry rustle, seventy, eighty yards to his right. There was a slight movement in the grass. He kept still, sweat making moist paths down his face, his neck, his back, his whole body. Then a bird made a harsh cheeping and set up from a position thirty yards away. Wolf knew he had got lucky. He took a chance. Fired. Then he was immediately rolling to change his position.

He heard the Indian give off a harsh gasp, then he popped up like a cork out of a bottle from the long grass. Blood smeared his tunic. The crazy bastard began running towards him fumbling for the knife in his wampum belt and singing a wild song. Wolf jacked in another load, to finish him, but the gun jammed.

Now the Indian was almost upon him. He was still chanting his weird song. His big knife was above his head, ready to strike down as he dived at him.

Wolf rolled. The Indian hit the ground with a solid thud, missing him. Wolf got to his feet, his blood racing and clubbed down with the rifle, smacking the metal-edged butt against the back of the Indian's head.

The redman's song died abruptly. Wolf felt sure the rifle's butt had cracked open the Indian's skull. But he struck down again until blood and brains were exposed and the Indian lay still. The countryside went deathly quiet once more.

Wolf looked up. The pinto was still standing where the Indian had left it. He stripped off the Indian's tunic, pulled it over his holed and ragged woollen jacket. He wanted the animal to respond quickly, no antics.

As he approached, the animal moved, but it had clearly scented the Indian's smell and was uncertain as to whether or not to bolt. The slight agitation the horse had, Wolf assumed, was probably down to the smell of the blood on the coat.

When he got close he took hold of the army bridle on it and eased himself into the army saddle. The beast was not altogether happy, but it allowed him to gently urge it to the base of the rock formation. Securing the reins under a heavy rock he gathered his belongings. He'd already observed there was a full waterskin on the pinto, plus a bag of what appeared to be a paste of meat and pulped fruit. A tentative taste proved it to be palatable.

Wolf allowed his elation full rein. He was still in business. He glanced east. He could see no dust yet, but he had no doubts there would be. The shot must have alerted them. He remounted the Indian's horse and lit out for the great spaces.

9

As Wolf began to move away from the escarpment the crack of rifles from the rimrock above and the thud of lead hitting the ground nearby sent him scurrying back to cover. As he looked up cautiously, his thoughts raced. It was rugged terrain up there, not easy for a horse and rider to move fast over. Down here, he had a clear run. A man would be a fool not to take advantage of the overhangs the cliff face offered.

Without hesitation, he urged the pinto into a gallop along the base of the ramparts. Half a mile on he cut out on to the grasslands. As he did, more rifle fire from the rim chattered spiteful noise. But it was frustrated fire. He knew he was out of range. Grim elation filled him. Once more he had out-smarted Fenger.

Feeling the sheer joy that knowledge brought, he headed toward the sun now sinking towards the western horizon. He still had this compulsion to go west — ever west, hoping to lose himself in its vastness and put an end to Fenger's relentless hounding. Then he could commence the hunt for the killers of his parents. He would not allow himself to consider failure in the almost impossible task he had set himself. Hadn't he found Zack Boles? Lucky, maybe, but . . .

Easing the pinto down he cantered it for most of what was left of the afternoon. All the time he rode, though, he could see big thunderheads building up to the south-east of him and vivid tongues of lightning flickering to earth out of their dark, brooding bellies. It looked like it was going to be a big storm, if it turned this way.

Topping a rise he paused, took out the telescope he had found in the beaded doeskin bag attached to the

Indian's saddle and scanned his back trail. As he searched he figured it would take Fenger some time to gather his men into something resembling a hunting pack once more. Already far behind him, the bulwark of rock he sought refuge on this morning was a dark bulk on the undulating prairie, shimmering in the heatwaves of the late afternoon.

Nevertheless, he was relieved to see his back trail was clear. But that didn't mean it would remain that way. He had long experience of Fenger. He was like a leech. He stuck and stuck, wouldn't let go. Wolf set his chin. However, there was one thing he could take comfort from — Fenger didn't have the Indian any more to do his tracking. In this country that could prove to be a big disadvantage, but Fenger had managed before. Wolf had no doubt the bastard would manage again.

He stowed the telescope, took a draught of water from the dead

Comanche's waterskin, wiped the perpetual sweat this country relentlessly drew out of him, then urged the pinto on.

As he rode he ate from the Indian's food supply. He discovered the fruitberry-and-meat paste was palatable and filling.

Now, as the last dregs of twilight — made lurid by the gathering storm — settled over the land, he found himself overlooking a shallow valley. It was plain it had been cut out of the prairie by the broad river which babbled through the dark screens of brush, cottonwoods and willows down there, now barely discernible to him in the closing dark. For some time he had been hearing the bawling of cattle. Now he saw them, spread out up the valley — a lot of them, made uneasy by the threatening storm. With sombre eyes, Wolf studied the beasts. A gather as large as this must mean there'd been organized herding. Was the person responsible for it Goodnight, the man

Benson talked of?

Using his knees he urged the Indian pinto along the ridge. Sure enough, maybe a mile ahead, he saw the faint glow of a camp-fire. And as he gazed, more thunder boomed out over the prairie, closer than ever. The force of it shook the earth and vivid lightning flickered down from the dark sky. He only needed one glance to tell him the storm was heading this way and if it broke near these cattle all hell could break loose.

He began to move around the mass of cows. He felt it reasonable to believe they were being held here overnight. And it didn't surprise him when a tall-hatted cowman came riding out of the gloom. What did surprise him, though, was the easily recognizable click of a weapon being fully cocked. Backing its deadly noise, the rider's order rang out clear, 'You-all hold it right there, stranger.'

Wolf raised his hands. 'I'm holdin'. No need fer the gun.'

'You figure?' The rider waved his Colt. 'I don't. Now move on down to the camp-fire. An' easy. Don't disturb the steers, they're tetchy enough.'

Without comment Wolf urged the pinto towards the bright, distant flicker. Five minutes later he and his gun guard rode into the fireglow. Wolf's keen gaze quickly took in the men sitting around it, eating off tin plates. They looked stern, mahogany-faced, tough men — obviously fashioned by the hard, uncompromising life they had chosen to follow. They'd stopped eating. Their alert, but not unfriendly stares, studied him.

From the background, a burly man with a dark-bearded, strong face, aged around thirty, Wolf judged, came from by an unusual wagon and approached them. The wagon had iron axles instead of wood, with a can of tallow hanging under it, clearly there for lubrication. It was canvas-covered and had a hinged shelf on the back, laid out with paraphernalia a cook would use in the preparation and serving of meals. A canvas hammock hung underneath the rig.

As the man walked towards the firelight, he emptied what remains of food there was on his plate on to the ground and dropped it into a tin bowl of water as he went past. Once more lightning flickered and thunder rolled. It caused all the eating men to stare grimly at the sky. As the man came close he said, 'Who've we got here, John?'

Behind him, Wolf heard the man de-cock his cap-and-ball Colt Navy and presumed he reholstered it. 'He was lookin' the herd over,' the rider said. 'I guessed you'd want to take a look at him.'

Wolf met the questioner's steady gaze as it turned on to him. Instantly he knew this man was the boss of the outfit. It showed in every fibre of his bearing. There was strong, stern power there, authority. This was a man who got things done and didn't let anything stand in his way while doing it.

He said, 'I'm Charles Goodnight. These here men are helping me to round up wild cattle to take to Fort Sumner. They have a need for beef up there. That said, what interest have you in the herd?'

By the look of him Wolf guessed Goodnight would accept only the truth and would quickly figure out you weren't telling it, if that was the case. 'Wolfgang Strange,' he said. 'I've come lookin' fer you. Benson at the crossin' spoke of you when I asked if he knew a place I could find work.'

Goodnight rubbed his bearded chin. 'I see.' Wolf saw the cattleman's keen gaze was taking in his Confederate campaign hat — the dirty, thin rope around it and the gold tassels still on it below the weathered CSA logo. 'You wouldn't be running from something, would you, Strange?' The men around, their leathery, weather-and-life-carved faces etched in the fireglow, leaned forward, victuals once more temporarily forgotten.

Wolf met their stares before swivelling his gaze back to Goodnight. He judged the cattleman was a man who had lived a rugged, independent life from an early age and wouldn't suffer fools gladly. But he seemed prepared to hear a man out when he asked him to talk. Wolf told his story from his parents' deaths onward, feeling that was the way Goodnight would want it. Finishing it off, he looked squarely at the cattleman. 'An' in thet, yuh've got the truth of it, Mr Goodnight. Take it or leave it.'

While he had spoken the rancher's gaze had narrowed, but his square face revealed nothing of what he might be thinking. He nodded and said, 'I'll take it. Missouri guerrilla, huh? Red Legs killed your Ma and Pa?' He rubbed his chin again, gaze still slitted. 'This Captain Fenger . . . he still dogging you?'

'I reckon so.'

Goodnight seemed to go into deep

thought then said, 'I, too, served the Rebel cause as a Texas Ranger' — he waved a hand about him — 'as did most of the men here, but that is over now and we have our fine, ravaged state of Texas to rebuild.' Strength and determination filled the cattleman's features. 'And, by God, we will do it, Strange. Be assured of that.' Goodnight's stare remained on him for a few more moments, then he peered forward. 'You ate recently?'

'Thet Injun I killed back there. Ate some of what I found in the bag he carried, though I got other vittles. I've kind of got expert at caterin' fer trouble.'

'Mind if I take a look at the Indian food?' Goodnight stepped forward.

Wolf offered the bag. Was Goodnight verifying his story, or just being curious? The cattleman said, 'Hum. Pemmican.' Then he looked at the smaller bag in which Wolf found the little telescope, amongst other strange-looking accoutrements. Goodnight looked into that too, then looked up. 'Comanche medicine bag,' he said. 'Well, I guess no Texican around here is going to git riled with a man who occasionally kills himself a Comanche.' The corners of his dark eyes crinkled and he stepped back. 'Dismount, Strange. Help yourself at the chuck-wagon.'

'Can I take it I got a job?'

Goodnight eyed him, clearly not altogether certain. 'You had dealings with mean cows that's spent five wild years in the brakes?'

Wolf shook his head. 'No, sir. On'y got knowledge of farm animals. But thet don't mean I can't learn.'

'You learn quick?'

'I learn quick.'

Goodnight nodded gravely. 'First, I will tell you my conditions of employment. With me there is no drinking and gambling on a drive and I will expect what orders I give to be carried out, though I will not ask any man to do anything I am not prepared to do myself.' His stare became keener. 'Will that be satisfactory to you?'

'Yes.'

Goodnight nodded. 'Good.'

Wolf now felt his very soul was being bared by Goodnight's probing stare as he continued to consider him. Then the cattleman said, 'OK, Strange, I'll give you a trial. But you will find this is no easy job you are about to embark upon.'

On the heels of Goodnight's words, more thunder raged with renewed vigour across the south-eastern sky and lightning momentarily defeated the camp-fire glow, bathing the grim faces of the men around it in a metallic glow. It caused them *and* Goodnight to again stare up at the dark canopy overhead. By their expressions they were clearly worried.

After moments of listening Goodnight said, 'I was going to suggest you get a good night's sleep before I explained what your pay and first duties will be, but by the sound of that, you may be thrown in at the deep end tonight.'

Wolf stared at the thick-set, intent man. 'Meanin'?'

Goodnight drew himself up tall, his stare hawk-like. 'Meaning we may have a stampede on our hands before this night is through, Strange. That is a dangerous thing. If you are called upon to help us turn it, my advice to you will be to keep in your saddle and stay on the flanks of the herd and with the rest of us help to try and head them off, get them circling on themselves — milling as we call it. D'you think you'll be able to cope with that?'

Wolf nodded. 'On'y one way to find out.'

Goodnight gave him another sharp look. 'Indeed there is.'

The cattleman then turned to a lanky, loose-limbed man who had just risen from the camp-fire, emptied his plate and put it in the water-filled bowl. 'Nate,' he said, 'saddle up another horse for me. Want to take a good look at the

herd. I don't like this smell in the air.'
Wolf caught Goodnight's glance as he
looked back at him over his shoulder.
'Bad storms have a smell all their own,
Strange. You know that?'

Wolf said, 'No. But I guess I know
what you're gettin' at.'

As he said it, the wind began gusting,
hissing through the grass, guttering the
flames of the camp-fire. Wolf felt it
flapping his ragged trousers against his
thin legs. Under him the dead Indian's
pinto began to move restlessly, sniffing
the air, twitching its ears and snorting.
Goodnight was already striding off into
the night.

Wolf climbed down. As he did, a
grizzled man wearing an apron came
down from the fancy wagon, carrying a
plate of beef hash. 'I'm the outfit's
cook, boy,' he said. 'This'll be the on'y
time yuh'll git yuh vittles handed to
you. So eat hearty. An', goin' on that
humdinger of a storm boilin' up, an'
the tetchiness of those cows down
yonder — though not wantin' to appear

gloomy, mind — it could be the last meal yuh'll ever have!' He wheezed a laugh, but Wolf saw the cook's grin was not altogether a hearty one, more a nervous giggle.

Accepting the food, he placed the plate down on the ground while he hitched the pinto to a rope line some fifty yards away, clearly rigged up as a tie point for range horses while the cowmen ate. It suggested they didn't anticipate getting much sleep this night.

While he hunkered down and ate, the cook began busying himself washing the plates dumped in the deep tin bowl and stacking them along with the rest of the stuff inside the strange wagon. As he worked, the cowhands passed over their plates and began heading for their tied-up mounts. Their talk was low, terse.

An hour later, the storm appeared to calm a little, veer off. Some riders came back into camp. Their mood was a little lighter. Talk was they thought it may have played itself out. Nevertheless, they continued on to the large remuda out on the range and roped out fresh mounts and headed on back into the night.

Meantime, Wolf watched as the cook completed loading up, hitched up four oxen to haul the chuckwagon, as he called it, then urged them into a grunting walk. As he went past he called, 'Git into the saddle an' stay there, boy, if you fancy holdin' on to your hide.'

Finding himself alone, Wolf stared after the lumbering wagon, but within a minute more riders came in. One steered his mount straight up to him. 'Yuh ridin' with me, Strange. Climb up an' stay close.'

Wolf mounted the Indian pinto and followed the man into the night. As he closed up on him he said, 'Figure we might be gittin' away with it?'

The short, wiry rider, who, like himself, couldn't be more than twenty or so, stared narrowly at him, his sunburned face hollow in what was left of the camp-fire. He spat. 'With cows, mister, wild or tame, you get to expect the unexpected. Jest bear that in mind.' He nudged his roan into a canter with his knees. The last remaining hand kicked out the fire and remounted.

As they'd rode towards the gather, a big moon got up, but it was continually obscured by heavy cloud. Wolf decided, belying the cowmen's edginess, all was uncannily peaceful and it wasn't long before the herd loomed out of the night. Wolf followed the rider as he began to circle the restless beasts.

Things appeared to be going fine. Wolf felt himself relaxing, thinking the cowmen were skittish about nothing. But it all started as if on a prearranged signal, worked out by the beeves. Close by, Wolf heard an old cow snuff loudly. Before he could take his next breath the whole herd was up and running, like all the hounds of hell had come up out of the ground and were snapping at their heels.

'Jesus, holy hell, boys,' his companion

cried, 'they're a'runnin'!'

Wolf caught his wild-eyed stare. 'Jest keep with 'em, Strange. Try an' head 'em off like Goodnight said. But fer Cris'sake, keep your saddle an' keep outa the middle. You hear me?'

Hardly taking in his advice, Wolf began to fight the Indian pinto. The herd's sudden unrest caused it to begin to lunge and neigh and panic. The night abruptly became full of the roar of thousands of pounding hooves, the clashing of a myriad of flashing, lethal longhorns.

Now, erupting all around Wolf, desperate yips and yells began punctuating the night. Men were whipping up their horses into a gallop to match the herd's run, guns popping their spiteful noise. Wolf went with them, electrified by the excitement that had suddenly exploded all around him. The raw power of the thundering cattle — their wild eyes glaring fearfully out of the night, their raucous bawling honking and confused. The flying turf, the dust — clouds of it rising up, choking and restricting their already night-limited vision.

Then, for a moment, even above all the calamitous dim around him, Wolf thought he heard the awful, despairing cries of men. Their harsh noise was coming from the head of the stampede. However, in the terrible din, the terrible shrieking was soon lost to Wolf in the ever-rising tumult around him and he paid it no more heed.

Getting the pinto to obey his hand once more he followed the cowmen into the night, drawing his belt gun and shouting at the thundering cattle. Then, abruptly, the rain started to slash down. With it, the thunder boomed like a cannon barrage across the sky and the white, vivid flashes of lightning which illuminated the devilish, awesome chaos of bawling hide and flesh in their frenzied rush, exposed what looked like a scene from Hell. And an intense stench of dirt, sulphur, cattle and raw fear began choking the air. He felt he could almost touch it as well as taste it.

His vision helped by the big moon, though obscured behind the lowering clouds, Wolf saw Goodnight come riding out of the night, through the lances of rain. He was waving a blanket. When the cattleman saw him he cut across to him. He roared, 'I am making for the head of the herd. Are you with me, Strange?'

Wolf knew it was a challenge. 'With you,' he bawled.

'Keep in that saddle,' Goodnight ordered above the din. 'Use your gun. Kill some if you have to, but do your damnedest to turn the herd.'

With that Goodnight began quirting his horse towards the head of the stampede. As they got close Wolf saw a big brindle bull was leading the charge, its huge spread of horns spread out like deadly blades of death. Wolf fired his Colt into the air, yelled until his throat and lungs threatened to give out. He soon found he had plunged himself into a nightmare madness of drenching rain, splattering mud and bawling cattle. Sometimes he came within a hair's-breadth of being skewered by horns or pulverized by the unceasing, pounding hooves. It was so totally different from the world he had known. And all the time he rode, Goodnight's instructions were banging in his head: 'Keep in your saddle. Turn the herd, turn the herd.' It began to seem to Wolf it was an impossible task; that it was a battle of titanic wills and the cows were winning.

Goodnight rode and bawled ahead of him, waving his blanket. The night around was chaos; the deluge of rain, cold and lashing — the thunder overhead roaring and crashing — the lightning illuminating the tight-packed, rain-shiny backs of men and animals with snake-tongue, deadly flickers.

Yet, all around Wolf, the cowboys were riding expertly, dangerously close, their faces grim, their guns blazing into the night. Some lashed out with long bullwhips at the running masses. But, to Wolf, it seemed it would go on for ever — with the cows running headlong into the night, heading for God knew where into God knew what. All he knew was he had to stick with them, turn them, turn them. Goodnight had said so.

Then it happened. Inexplicably, the head of the herd began swinging, running back on itself until it was racing round, tightening up, bawling and fighting and milling, splashing through the huge pools of rain that had formed in the hollows of the grasslands.

Dawn came in bright, calm and clear. It revealed to Wolf dismal, sodden, appalling sights. Carcasses, mostly old cattle and calves, strewn about, the dawn punctuated by the sound of guns destroying animals because of broken limbs or crushed bodies, but not yet dead. Cattle stood, heads hung, bewildered by the recent madness — steaming and exhausted.

Beside him, erect in his saddle, staring long at the death and devastation around him, Goodnight turned to him They had both changed their played-out horses at the remuda an hour back. Miraculously, cook had coffee ready for the boys as they came dribbling in to change mounts. Wolf found Goodnight's steady gaze had altered little from last night, despite the savage consequences of the stampede he had been studying. A setback, but, undaunted, he would go on was Wolf's impression. Goodnight nodded, with a sort of curt movement and searched his face with keen eyes. 'Well, by God, you'll do, Strange,' he said. 'Now, we've got to begin to count the cost of all this, organize and start again. This herd must be got to Fort Sumner.'

Wolf stared at him, his feelings of respect ever-growing. He wanted to help this man get his cattle to the fort in New Mexico Territory. But, almost on cue, as if it was a recurring nightmare and to frustrate his dream, Fenger's familiar, upright and immaculately uniformed frame at the head of his Red Legs began to loom in his mind's-eye now the excitement of the stampede was over. His stomach clenched in frustration. God damn them.

Snapping him out of it, Goodnight swung his mount to the right and urged it forward. 'Accompany me, Strange,' he said, in a tone that brooked no argument. As Wolf turned with the cattleman, a rider came running his mud-splattered horse out of the, at present, steam-shrouded prairie, already drying fast under the increasingly hot sun. He slewed his mount to a stop in the wet soil by them. He was clearly agitated.

'You got to see this, Mr Goodnight.'

Goodnight frowned. It was an annoyed frown. 'What have I got to see, Cameron? Damn it, explain yourself.'

The rider's gaze was hollow and round. 'Back in the valley where we bedded down the herd. Dead men.

Must have got caught up in the stampede.'

Goodnight's annoyance left him immediately to be replaced with concern. 'This is grave news.' He turned his horse. 'Strange, come with us.'

They found the herd had run a long way. Last night's bed-down site was now a ten mile ride to the rear. Throughout the ride they galloped over hoof-chewed devastation. As they neared the bed-down site a hand came down off the valley ridge to await their arrival. When they got to him he was sitting his saddle, smoking his pipe. He pointed down at three bodies.

'Thet's all there is, Mr Goodnight,' he said.

Goodnight nodded, grimly. It was clear the corpses had been pulled to this spot from the positions in which they met their terrible end. Their horses, crushed into extinction, were left where they lay.

Wolf dismounted and followed

Goodnight to the mangled men. Though he was hardly recognizable, Wolf finally came to the conclusion the one he was staring down at was Captain Fenger. His usually immaculate uniform was plastered with mud, ripped and bloodied; pounded — as was his body — by the hooves of many cattle. The other two were Red Legs. No other members of Fenger's troop were in sight, suggesting they were scattered and had just kept riding. But upon seeing the corpses, Wolf's mind harked back. Had those stark cries he had heard in the night at the start of the stampede been the death cries of these men?

Wolf turned to Goodnight and pointed. 'Thet's Captain Fenger. He must have seen your fire and was heading towards it when the cows began to run.'

Goodnight's gaze, as usual, was level and calm. 'You are certain of this?'

Wolf nodded. 'No doubts.'

Goodnight shook his head solemnly.

'I can only say this is no way for a man to die.'

Wolf raised dark brows. 'No, sir. It ain't.'

Goodnight's stare was quick, searching. 'Considering your experiences regarding Fenger, your response surprises me, Strange.'

Wolf shrugged. 'He had been given a job to do. Get me and my men. His superiors had decided the war wasn't over fer us. Because of that, it also made sure the war wasn't over for the captain, either. In one way, I admired Fenger. He was a determined soldier. That is not to say I wouldn't have killed him on sight had I got the chance.'

Goodnight nodded. 'A man has the right to think that way when faced with such danger.' He gazed about him. 'It looks as though his men have dispersed, or gone for help.' Goodnight paused, rubbed his stubbled chin, lapsed into what seemed deep thought for a moment, then said, 'I think we'll need

210

to keep you out of sight until I get things cleared up with Major Bryant — he's the commander of the Federal post they've set up at Benson's Crossing. Perhaps it might be best if we found you dead, too, and buried you as well.' Wolf met his quizzical gaze. 'How d'you feel about that?'

Wolf stared. 'If you mean what I think you mean there's on'y one answer to that, but I got to ask why.'

Goodnight smiled. 'For me, it's quite simple: the war is over. It's time men were left to pick up their lives again . . . in peace.' The rancher lifted his chin. 'I'll put you with two of my *vaqueros*. With them you can engage yourself in helping with the rounding-up and learning of cows until we are ready to head for Fort Sumner. Are we agreed?'

Wolf held Goodnight's steady gaze. It clearly invited no refusal. 'Agreed,' Wolf said. 'An' I'm beholden.'

Goodnight smiled for a second time. 'Don't be,' he said. 'You will herd cows for me to Fort Sumner, Strange, because you have agreed to do so. And maybe, before this drive is through, you'll probably be wishing to God you'd headed straight for Mexico.'

10

Whilst gathering the herd in Texas, Wolf discovered Charles Goodnight had a partner, Oliver Loving, who joined Goodnight on the trail with more cattle to add to the herd. When the two considered they had sufficient, they swung the herd south to avoid the attentions of the ever-marauding Comanche, then forced them across the waterless Staked Plains to the Horse-head Crossing of the Pecos.

As they drew close to the river, the thirsty cattle got whiff of the water. They became uncontrollable. In the rush, several steers drowned and the river was blocked for a while by their jammed bodies. It took a deal of hard work to regather the maddened beasts and sort out the mess.

After three days' rest, they turned the 2,000 half-wild cattle north, following the Pecos, fording the river at Pope's Crossing, then pushed on to Fort Sumner. The herd comprised 1,200 steers, the rest stock cattle. At the fort the government contractor would not take the cows, but paid eight cents a pound on the hoof for what steers they had; an almost unprecedented price. The expression on Goodnight and Loving's faces made it plain they were greatly pleased with the transaction. And, having got to know them purty well on the drive, Wolf decided their reaction to the influx of such wealth was predictable: Goodnight was going back to Texas to amass another herd, while Loving was to take the remaining cattle on to Denver to sell them there.

The celebrations of their arrival at Fort Sumner over, out on the range with the resting stocker cattle before they were to be driven on to Denver, Wolf — now filled out and ruggedly healthy after two months of regular food and gruelling long hours in the saddle — gazed at Goodnight. The rancher's face expressed his disappointment.

He sighed. 'Can't I persuade you to stay with us, Strange? As I have already made known to you, myself and Mr Loving have big plans to expand our enterprises. And some day soon I intend to start ranching in Colorado — there is much virgin graze up there — to add to the holding I already have by Bosque Grande on the Pecos.'

As he spoke, Goodnight's look became earnest. 'Damn it, I need trustworthy men and I now know you have that quality in abundance. I'll make no bones about it, you could make a good career with me. You have courage, intelligence and determination. I believe being put to eventually running one of my establishments will not be beyond your capabilities and I have plans to do that in the not too distant future.'

Wolf pursed his lips. 'It ain't thet I'm not tempted, Mr Goodnight, but I guess the answer still has to be no.'

Goodnight made an imploring movement with a powerful right arm. 'I'm offering you a career, Strange. I'll make no bones about it, you could be making a big mistake.'

'You could be right,' admitted Wolf.

The flush that came to Goodnight's rugged face showed his frustration. 'Damn it, man . . . ' He made efforts to calm himself before saying, 'I don't wish to pry into your affairs, Strange, but I feel I have to. Is it the need to avenge your parents that is preventing you seizing this opportunity?'

Wolf set his stubborn jaw. 'Yes.'

Goodnight breathed hard down his nose. Wolf knew it wasn't often the rancher took so much interest in a man and he felt flattered, as well as a little ungrateful. Goodnight said, 'I know such terrible things can be hard to swallow, but could you not look upon their demise as a sad misfortune of war?

This lust for vengeance is not pretty and . . . have you thought of this? The men you seek could already be dead, having not survived the war. You know, it takes a real big man to forgive and forget a wrong done, Strange. Think on that.'

Wolf gazed steadily at the rancher, not offended by his words for he knew they were meant well. He had grown to like and respect Charles Goodnight and he had gathered through brief comments over the past two months, the rancher had come to have regard for him. He said, feeling a little wretched, 'It ain't thet I don't want to take up your offer, sir, I truly do. But it's somethin' I have to do. I won't be able to rest until I have.'

Once more Goodnight sighed heavily, tightened his lips, stared hard and shook his head. After moments of clear unhappiness, the rancher extended his hand. 'Very well, if that is your decision. Nevertheless, I think you have set yourself an almost insurmountable task. You have no names to go on and this whole vast country to search. Have you any plans as to where to start?'

Wolf raised dark brows. 'Not yet.'

Goodnight pursed his lips. 'In that case, can I suggest something?'

'I'm open to ideas.'

'The goldfields of Colorado,' said Goodnight. 'Though they've been booming for some time, now the war is over they'll be luring war-deprived men in droves, hungry for riches, a better life. Perhaps you may find luck there.' A rare smile played along the rancher's firm lips. 'Also, to make your journey profitable, you could help Mr Loving to push these cows on to Denver.' He nodded at the grazing herd.

Wolf grinned along with him. You had to hand it to Goodnight: he never gave up. He raised his dark brows. It was a tempting offer, but he was restless to begin the hunt and didn't want to be delayed by droving more cattle. Nevertheless, he turned Goodnight's suggestion over in his mind. He reckoned there was one possible flaw the rancher's analysis of what the men he sought might be doing, accepting they were alive, that is. His own view was: first, they would be greedy, ruthless men, looking for quick riches. Second, they would be prepared to kill and steal for wealth rather than earn it by honest means.

'I guess you've given me a place to start, Mr Goodnight,' he said, 'but, again, I must turn down your offer to help drive the stocker herd there.'

Goodnight squared his shoulders and looked genuinely thwarted, but he quickly seemed to shrug the refusal off. 'A great pity, Strange,' he said. He unpuckered his brow and added briskly, 'Well, no matter.' Another grin. '*Vaja con Dios*, my friend. If you ever need a job, look me up.' As if he had dismissed the whole matter from his mind he strode off towards the chuckwagon.

A day later, victuals stowed and riding out of Fort Sumner, the pinto moving at a comfortable gait, Wolf became increasingly sympathetic to Goodnight's advice regarding where to start his search. It could prove to be sound. And he was not short of means to sustain a long campaign. He had the wherewithal left from the guerrilla days, plus the money he had earned on the drive to Fort Sumner. And the anonymity that resulted from Goodnight's word that the notorious Wolf Strange was no more being accepted at the Benson's Crossing army post by Major Bryant was a bonus.

When he hit Denver he found a bustling, wide-open town spread across the confluence of the South Platte and Cherry Creek. Gold and silver was making it rip-roaring prosperous. Brick buildings were replacing most of the wooden structures. Once, on the trail, when in a yarning mood, Goodnight talked about Colorado in general and Denver in particular. He talked about the big fire of 1860, that wiped out most of the old town. Now it looked as though they intended to make a real permanent place of it, judging by the brick structures around.

He put up at a small hotel on one of the lesser streets and after a hearty supper walked out to tour the drinking places. Near midnight he was sick of staring at faces, sick of drinking rotgut whiskey — though his intake had been small — sick of brawling, drunken miners, though their boisterous behaviour wouldn't have bothered him normally. He finally realized his big trouble was, he was sorely missing the peace of the big range, the calm steadfastness of the men he'd worked with, the challenge of driving cattle across vast, trackless country and the hopelessness of his quest.

Stepping out of the saloon, he found the comparative quiet of the night and cool smack of air coming in from the mountains refreshing. Its tingle was welcome after an evening breathing the fug of tobacco smoke, the reek of booze, the cheap perfume of the barroom floozies. But he was irritable. Yes, the whole idea he could find the men he sought was beginning to convince even him how crazy the notion was, how futile the search would be. As Goodnight had pointed out, they were probably dead, or dispersed to God knew where. He could go on for ever and find nothing . . . just gradually grow more bitter, more warped in his thinking with each disappointment. The rancher was right. War left terrible things in its wake. A man had to put them behind him, restart his life, allow his grief to fade. Goodnight had already given him the opportunity to do so by, first, killing him off as far as the Kansas authorities were concerned, and second, by inviting him to stick with him and thoroughly learn the ins and outs of the cattle business, then go on to assume greater responsibilites.

'Mister, you got a light?'

Wolf stared at the fat, swaying man before him, his features indistinct in the faint yellow light the nearby, guttering street coal-oil lamp gave. He was clearly half-drunk. He was holding a cigar near his mouth and was gazing at him with bleary eyes.

'Sure.' Wolf found a sulphur match and wiped it up his broadcloth trousers. In the light it gave, as the man sucked life into his cigar amid clouds of smoke, Wolf realized he recognized certain things about his beard-grizzled features. He came to the abrupt conclusion he last saw this man hunched down in his saddle, blood oozing out of his shot-peppered trousers. He had been sitting his horse, standing off on the trail from Pa's homestead — near the bridge they'd made, while the man about to kill him lined up his Colt to put in the final, killing bullet. Wolf felt a sensation like ice-cold water trickle down his backbone.

The stranger grinned, waved his cigar. 'Much obliged, mister. Now, you gotta let me buy you a drink. See, me an' my pard hev' hit it real big Central

City way and seein' you have a real friendly face, not like some of the miserable bastards I seen around here, includin' my pard, I figure you'll be good company. An', damn it, I git the feelin' I seen you before some place. The war, maybe? Am I right?'

'It could be,' Wolf said. He could hardly contain his excitement. But it was a deadly excitement that crawled deep in his gut.

He felt the man's heavy arm drape across his shoulders. His breath was rank. The old pals routine sent shivers through Wolf. Automatically, his body tensed up, like drawn up fence-wire, because of his suspicions about him. But he didn't question his good fortune. Pa had always said: 'Remember, God can move in mysterious ways, son.' Wolf blinked. It appeared, this time, Pa was right. However, he had to be sure, very sure, this was one of the men he sought.

He allowed the stranger to heave him into the nearest saloon. He couldn't help but notice the man favoured his right leg.

The calico queens always knew a sucker when they saw one and the stranger became a prime target right off. Delighted with their interest, he called for champagne. As the cork popped loudly, shrieks of excitement came from the young girl the man had already coiled his brawny arm around. Then, with his free hand, the stranger filled glasses and offered them around. Wolf took his with a grin which had no humour in it. As if on cue, the jangle of the piano started once more, clearly the pianist having been out back attending to a call of nature, or maybe something else. The crowded saloon livened up. A miner started up a song to accompany the pianist. Soon others joined in.

Beaming, the stranger drank heartily and said, 'Won't stand on ceremony, pardner. I'm Bone Head Jimmy Gains. Whut's your handle, if it ain't too impolite to ask?'

'Wolf Strange.' Wolf waited for a

reaction. None came.

Bone Head raised his glass. 'Well, Wolf, here's mud in your eye.' He tossed back the sparkling drink, then surveyed Wolf with a bleary gaze while also leering a grin. 'Ain't you gittin' yourself a little lady, too?'

Wolf held down his growing loathing for this blustering sot. If he was one of the men he sought he wanted names, *all* the names. 'Not tonight, Jimmy. I'm a little tired, I guess. Had a long ride today. Jest got into town.'

Bone Head looked disappointed. 'God damn, you ain't goin' to act up on me like my pard, are you?'

'Guess so.'

'Hell, you can sleep all day tomorrow, can't yuh? Damn it, life's too short.' Gains grinned at the girls sharing his champagne, hugged the one he had his arm around. 'Ain't thet right, sweetheart?'

One painted lady sidled forward, draped a white, flabby arm around Wolf's neck. The smell of her cheap perfume was nauseating. 'I can help you sleep real good, cowboy . . . after we've played around a little, that is,' she said. 'You rode in to dig for gold?'

'Jest weighin' up the options,' Wolf said. He sipped his champagne and smiled.

'Oh hell, relax, Wolf,' Bone Head said. 'I thought I'd dropped on a real pal to drink with in you, but, God damn, you want to sleep, too.'

'Your friend got a name, too, Jimmy?' Wolf said.

Bone Head hiccupped. 'Why, sure. Maybe you heard o' him. Kelsy Jaul. Now, what the hell do yuh make of a name like thet? I ask yer. *Kelsy Jaul.*'

For effect, Wolf grinned. 'Sure is different.'

Bone Head nodded. 'You kin say thet agin, by God.' He poured more champagne for himself and the girls and drank loudly, then ordered more.

Wolf stared, as if curious. 'You in the war, Jimmy?'

'Sure.' He pointed a fat, grubby

227

finger. 'An' I figure thet's where I seen you.' Bone Head's eyes rounded, looked surprised. 'But, hell, what red-blooded man wasn't?' He lifted his right leg. 'Git this all shot up.' He gazed unsteadily at Wolf's Reb hat. 'My figurin' wasn't wrong; you were, too, right?'

'Right.'

Bone Head wobbled a little while gazing at him. It would have been a good attempt at a shrewd look but for his apparent advanced intoxication. 'Reckon, because o' thet, you can shoot purty good, too, huh?' he said. As if to emphasize his point he waved his finger at Wolf's two Colt Armys; one in the holster, one in his belt.

'I can take care of myself,' Wolf said.

'An' you come lookin' fer gold?'

Wolf grinned, disarmingly. 'A man has to keep his options open.'

As if sobered a little, Bone Head gazed steadily. 'Options, huh? Well, I know a leetle about options myself.' He switched his stare to the girls, fawning around him. He dropped dollars on the bar. 'Champagne's ordered. He'p yerself, ladies. Ol' Bone Head'll be back soon, then we'll hev' some real fun. Git a leetle business to talk over with my pardner here first.'

Wolf allowed Gains to steer him to a free table. Bone Head carried what remained of the first bottle with him. He filled his glass and waved the bottle at Wolf. Wolf shook his head and said, 'Maybe tomorrow, Jimmy. You said you got business . . . '

Suddenly, Bone Head's inebriation rolled off him like water. 'So, whut outfit you ride with in thet war, Wolf?'

'How about the Missouri Raiders?'

Bone Head's eyes narrowed; his beefy face became taut; his bleary gaze cleared swiftly. 'Yeah. By God. Wolf Strange. Real bad outfit, right? Heard tell they'd kilt you an' your boys off, down in Texas.'

'Rumour gits it wrong, sometimes.'

Bone Head scrubbed his grizzled chin. 'Seems thet way. So . . . you're on the run? Right?'

'Wrong.' Wolf grinned a mirthless grin. 'It's clear you ain't heard I was killed in a stampede.'

Bone Head's fat, bristly face lit up. He gulped champagne. 'God help me, you could be jest what me an' my pards are lookin' fer. We're gittin' an operation goin'. Could pay off real swell.' Gains revealed brown, rotting teeth in a wolfish smile. 'So far me an' Kelsy, we jest bin rollin' miners fer their paydirt.'

'In Central City?'

'Yeah, but it got a leetle hot.'

Wolf narrowed his eyelids. 'You said a *new* operation?'

Bone Head grinned some more. 'Uh huh, an' you is trained right up fer it, bein' a guerrilla an' all, is what I'd say. You hev' any hang-ups about workin' with some Kansas boys of like nature?'

Wolf shrugged. 'No hang-ups. But, I gotta disappoint you, pard. I've done with thet stuff.'

Bone Head raised his dark brows.

'Thet so? Well, I don't want to be unfriendly, friend, but admittin' thet around my pard might be a mistake when we meet up.'

Wolf felt his gut tighten up. 'Meanin'?'

Bone Head rasped his bristles. 'Though it ain't likely — you savvy? — sayin' you don't want to hear us out might result in trouble. Right?'

Wolf decided Bone Head Jimmy Gains had about as much finesse as a bull let loose among a rangeful of cows on heat. Wolf forced a grin. 'You tryin' blackmail on me, Jimmy? Now, thet sure ain't friendly, jest when I was beginnin' to take a shine to *you*.'

Bone Head grinned disarmingly, waved the brawny arm with the glass in it. 'Hell, I wouldn't do it, pardner, you know thet. Jest sayin' what could be if things didn't work out 'tween us. My pard, Kelsy's, total opposite to me. A real mean piece o' work. Wouldn't be surprised if he didn't jest up an' kill you if you decided what we got in mind weren't fer you. Security, yuh understand.'

Wolf restrained his growing revulsion. When the time came, it was going to be a pleasure killing this scum. But first, he had to get to know Kelsy Jaul — find out if he had been a member of the gang — and to get out of Gains the name of the last one of this devil's brood he was searching for, apart from Mitch Layton. He was going to play along, no matter how much it galled him, or how much it stuck in his craw to keep up this sickening charade.

Wolf took a sip at his champagne. 'Whut's to say I ain't a mean piece o' work, too, Jimmy?'

Bone Head grinned again, all friendly and happy. 'Hell, God damn it, thet's jest what we want, pard, so's you'll fit in our plans.'

'You mentioned another *hombre* about to ride in,' Wolf said. *Hombre* was a word he'd picked up from the Texas cowmen and it slipped out naturally.

Bone Head looked vacant. '*Hombre?*'

'Man.'

Gains grinned again. 'Oh. Yeah. Well, he'll be leadin' the outfit.' Bone Head's grey, bleary stare became hard. 'You about to take a dislike to thet?'

'Jest curious.'

Wolf decided Bone Head was taking it for granted he'd probably got a recruit for what was beginning to become clear through their clumsy conversation — Bone Head and Kelsy Jaul were in the throes of forming a gang of road agents. They'd seen there was good pickings to be had here amongst the goldfields and had informed the man coming riding in of a lucrative situation here, prime for plucking. Recruits, meantime, were being enlisted. What had made Bone Head pick on him? Wolf knew his mean look, acquired through the desperate border years, did make him appear to fit the part.

He smiled, slowly, then said, 'You know, Jimmy, you done read my future intentions, clean as a whistle. I'd figured there could be some rich pickin' around here as well.'

Bone Head beamed. 'So, God damn it, I wus right. Wolf, pard, we jest got to hev' thet drink. Yuh can't go off a'sleepin'.'

Wolf decided now, if he was going to get the identities of all the men who had killed his parents, he had to play this up to the hilt. He clapped Bone Head on his beefy shoulders and grinned into his sweaty face. 'Hell, why not . . . pardner?'

11

Wolf woke with a raging thirst and a thumping head. Buried in the blankets beside him, the girl there was purring small, contented snores. He didn't even remember going to bed with her. He must have passed into deep slumber as soon as he hit the pillows.

He slid out from between the sheets. She must have stripped off his guns and coat and taken off his boots before she'd heaved him into bed. She didn't look big enough to do that. But, he knew, women were deceptive, capable of more than they were given credit for. He hoped she wasn't too disappointed in other ways . . .

He checked his money belt. All there, which surprised him. Dressed, he laid a dollar on the small dressing-table and stepped out on to the gloomy landing. Downstairs in the saloon, he found

Bone Head eating breakfast. Ham and eggs, wallowing in grease, a pot of coffee. When Wolf saw the meal he felt he wanted to heave, but he decided to have the same. He needed something to chase the rotgut out of his system, line his queasy stomach. He ordered the meal from the brawny, heavy-lidded barman who had left off swamping the floor to come over and ask for his order.

When Wolf joined him, Bone Head was chipper. 'You look daid on your feet, pardner,' he leered, raised his eyebrows knowingly. 'You overdone it with the leetle lady? Haw, haw, haw.'

Wolf forced a smile. 'It could be.' He couldn't admit that he wasn't used to strong liquor, or had yet to experience more intimate things. In many ways he knew he was still a callow, inexperienced youth.

'Could be, hell,' Bone Head scoffed. 'She's drawn you off real good, boy. I can tell. Yuh can't pull the wool over this man's eyes.' After emitting another ribald guffaw he turned his attentions to his meal once more.

When his own food arrived, Wolf attacked it with similar gusto. He was picking his teeth when a miserable-looking man entered the saloon, the batwings squeaking noisily as they flapped together again behind him. But Wolf immediately knew the face. He tensed. *Number two.*

Bone Head looked up and grinned at the newcomer. 'Waal, howdy, Kelsy.' He downed the last of his fourth cup of coffee — coffee, Wolf found, you could stand a spoon up in.

As Kelsy Jaul approached, Wolf recognized the sallow, mean face and buck teeth, the blue eyes set too close together.

'We should be out the shack,' Kelsy Jaul said. 'You an' your damned women an' your damned drink. Hetch said to lay low. Stay outa trouble.'

Wolf caught Bone Head's grin as he turned to him. 'See what I mean, Wolf? Friendly as a polecat.'

'If you say so,' said Wolf.

He saw Jaul's stare was quick, mean as it darted to him, then returned to Bone Head. 'Who the hell's this?'

Still grinning Bone Head said, 'This here's Wolf Strange.'

Jaul stepped back immediately, his hand edging for his new single action Colt .45. 'You crazy . . . you gone loco?'

Bone Head appeared delighted he had startled Jaul. 'Even worse'n thet, Kelsy,' he said. 'He's gonna join us.'

Jaul kept his appalled stare on Gains. 'You dumb bastard. What you bin sayin' to him?'

'Nothin' to worry about,' Bone Head reassured. 'That'll come later, when Hetch looks him over.' Wolf caught Jimmy's stare as it switched on to him. It was laced with seriousness. 'An' he *will* look you over, pardner.' That said, Gains leaned back in his chair and belched expansively as he returned his gaze to Jaul. 'Truth is, Kelsy, we git a real mean man here. An' he's lookin' fer excitement, jest like us.'

Jaul glowered, his doubt clear. 'Mean? Shit! Hetch said wait. He'll do the pickin'.'

'Wait fer what?' said Bone Head. 'Ain't no wrong in recruitin', ifen the right man comes along.' Gains nodded knowingly. 'You allus been the same, Kelsy. Yuh hev' to be instructed in every damn move you make. Hetch'll be pleased we bin doin' somethin' to hurry things along. Bet your sweet ass on thet.'

Wolf met Jaul's cold, beady stare as he turned to him. 'Strange, you come out to the shack with us.'

'What I had in mind,' said Wolf. 'No need to git all riled up.'

Kelsy's stare continued. 'You reckon, huh? We'll see 'bout thet when Hetch arrives.' He turned to Bone Head. 'He wired to say he'll be here today.' Kelsy waved a yellow piece of paper under Jimmy's nose. 'While you bin whorin', I bin workin'.'

Bone Head's eyes rounded. He looked disappointed. 'Hell. Comin' today? I still got things to do. There's a leetle lady — '

Jaul thumped the top of the table. 'God damn. Save it. Noon stage. Hetch wants us to be there. Got it?'

After a moment of gloom, Bone Head's grin once more spread right across his face. He beamed first at Wolf, then at Jaul. 'Then, if that's so, there'll be a wild time in the old town tonight, boys. Like any man, Hetch likes a swallow of whiskey an' a roll with a woman. After thet — an' not before — if I know Hetch a'tall, the business will start.' He blinked at Wolf, his round face sweaty. 'So, you still of a mind, pardner? Like I said, Hetch ain't me. He'll want to look yuh over *real* good.'

Wolf smiled. 'Still of a mind. I need some action. Things ain't been too good of late fer me. One thing I did find out, drovin' cows is fer suckers, 'less you own the herd. I need some real money . . . quick.'

Bone Head beamed at Jaul and

belched. 'Yuh see, Kelsy? Keen an' mean.'

Jaul stared. 'Sayin's easy, doin's another thing. Let's git to the shack. Three hours it'll be noon. Then we'll see 'bout Strange.'

Following Jaul out and judging by the last few minutes, Wolf came to the firm conclusion that the blue-eyed, buck-toothed bastard bore watching, even if, as Bone Head intimated, he wouldn't make a move without directions from 'Hetch', or was reluctant to do so.

At the shack, ten minutes' walk from the expanding town's edge, Wolf cleaned up in the creek the rented cabin stood near and shaved, but made sure he was never far from his guns.

After an hour and a half, in which Bone Head snored on one of the three dirty bunks in the hut, they returned to town. Because they were passing the livery stable in which Wolf had stalled his horse, he looked in on it. He found it was in good shape. Gains and Jaul accompanied him. Jaul made it plain through his actions he was still far from accepting him and intended to keep both eyes fully on him.

Bone Head said, 'Thet an' Injun hoss?'

Wolf nodded. 'Got him off a Comanche who died on me. Lead poisonin'.'

Bone Head hooted with delight and batted Jaul on his narrow back. 'Yuh hear thet? Like I said, boy: mean.'

Jaul snorted his contempt. 'Jest a damned hoss. Let's git. Be damn well noon before we know it.' He threw a glare at Bone Head. 'Yuh know what Hetch'll be like ifen we turn up late.'

At the stage office, they made themselves comfortable on the bench outside. Wolf was thankful for the wooden awning above the boardwalk, which shaded him from the still hot sun overhead, despite summer coming swiftly to a close. As they waited, traffic of all kinds rumbled and squeaked up and down the thoroughfare, creating a constant haze of dust.

After half an hour, Bone Head moaned, 'Hell, I'm hungry. The God damned stage. What time you say it was supposed to git in, Kelsy?'

Jaul glowered. 'I tol' you . . . noon.'

Groaning impatiently, Bone Head reared up from his seat and looked in through the clean stage office windows. 'Clock in there says twelve-thirty. God damn it, they ever run on time? Wolf, what do you figure?'

Wolf shrugged, grinned, though it was becoming a big strain to do so. 'Looks like they don't,' he said, and settled back to watch the traffic some more.

All morning he conversed very little. He felt deep in his gut 'Hetch' would be the real polecat in this woodpile. Another thing, he didn't want to get too familiar with men he was going to kill. Hetch seemed to be their leader. Jaul was just a mean little bastard who took orders. Bone Head was at pains to give the impression he fitted his nickname, but Wolf didn't accept for one moment that that was the case with the bluff ex-Jayhawker. There was a coyote meanness slumbering deep in Bone Head Jimmy Gains. But, by the minute, he was feeling ever more sure that when the noon stage did finally roll in, the supreme nemesis in all this would alight from it. Wolf felt his gut tighten up, a nervous tic start in his right cheek.

After ten minutes of fidgeting silence Bone Head said, 'To hell with waitin'. I'm goin' to eat.' He stared. 'You comin', Wolf?'

Wolf gazed up at the fat man. 'Naw. I'll wait it out with Kelsy. Kind of curious about this here Hetch. He got another name?'

'Sure,' said Bone Head. 'Kinder.'

Jaul scowled bad-temperedly at Gains. 'God, you're like a damned hog. Can't you fergit your belly fer once?'

Bone Head glowered, showing his first sign of irritation. 'Better than bein' a miserable, scrawny sonofabitch like you.'

Jaul stiffened, reared, edged for his

Colt. 'Don't push it, Bone Head.'

For a moment, deadly scorn filled Bone Head's beefy, bristled features, then he relaxed. 'You'll do nothin', Kelsy. Hetch ain't given you his orders yit.'

Guffawing at that, Gains headed off across the road to the Lucky Dragon Eatery. He crowded in through the door with a bunch of carousing miners who arrived about the same time as himself.

Wolf was happy to sit and be silent with the brooding Kelsy Jaul. Ten minutes later Jaul erupted. He got up and stamped into the office bawling, 'When is the God damned stage gonna git in?'

'When it gets here,' came the dry reply from the clerk behind the counter.

Jaul returned and sat down heavily. 'God damned smart-ass sonofabitch.'

Fifteen minutes later the stage rocked in and stopped amid clouds of dust. Tense now, Wolf stood up with Jaul. Jaul leaned forward expectantly, blinking hooded lids over blue eyes.

Passengers began to get out, one lady pausing by the coach, obviously looking for somebody who was going to meet her. She was soon reassured when a smiling man stepped forward and kissed her, then they waited until the driver began handing down luggage.

Last of all Hetch Kinder stepped down. Immediately, Wolf's gut clenched and the years of mourning and pain fell away to be replaced with deadly intent. He would know *that* face anywhere: brutish features; red hair; big, thick-set body; grey, piercing eyes.

Those horrendous moments of three years ago that shattered his life came rushing back with crystal clarity as, once more, Kinder was leering down at him in the dismal, drear rain, his long-barrelled cap-and-ball Remington pointing right at him. Once more Wolf heard the shocking explosions as Kinder fired at him, felt the impact and the searing pain of the lead as it entered him.

Balling his fists, Wolf shut out the images, stared at his quarry. Kinder was in a blue string tie, dark, pinstripe suit and fancy boots. Unsurprisingly, the two Remington cap-and-ball six-guns he remembered were in black leather holsters, one on each hip. Kinder carried a new Winchester repeating rifle in his left hand.

Jaul stepped forward, waving a hand to attract his attention. 'Hetch! Over here.'

Kinder's stare turned and took them in. Immediately, Wolf locked his icy glare into Kinder's grey, cold look. Kinder's gaze instantly became suspicious, knowing. Wolf thought: It's coming back, huh, you bastard?

Kelsy Jaul was bleating, 'This here's Wolf Strange, Hetch. Hell, thet dumb shit Bone Head — '

Without taking his eyes off Wolf, Kinder raised a quieting hand. 'I know who it is.' He smiled, a panther smile. 'Well . . . finally come to collect, boy?'

Wolf said, 'I reckon. Who killed my Pa, Kinder?'

Kinder grinned some more. 'I did. Dragged him all around the damned farm, 'til he was raw meat. He was still alive when I cut his dick off. Wanna know why I did? He crossed me once, boy. Now, a man jest don't do thet to Hetch Kinder. Sooner or later he's git to pay. Thet Beely Valley raid gave me the perfect chance, the one I'd looked fer, fer ten years. He wus allus so damned *right*, your Pa. Now, looks like, I got a chance to put away his pup an' finish the job.'

Wolf controlled his cold anger. 'My Ma? You kill her, too?'

Kinder shook his head. 'Nooo. It was Kelsy here, Bone Head Jimmy Gains an' Mitch Layton, though Layton showed no real stomach fer it. In the end I did kind of pop off some lead, to put her out of her misery.' He grinned more. 'Damn it, even I have *some* humanity.'

Jaul made a strangled cry. Wolf

248

turned to see he was already moving, clawing for his fancy new Colt .45 while bawling, 'God damn you, Hetch. Need you ha' tol' him all o' thet?'

As Jaul shifted his stance, Wolf flung himself to the left and dropped to the boardwalk, pulling one of his Colt Armys as he did. Around him, women began screaming, men began pulling them away, crouching and running for cover.

None of the erupting pandemonium around him penetrated Wolf's deadly concentration. His first shot hit Jaul, sending him staggering back against an awning support. Jaul began yelling, blood spurting from his gut. His lead broke the stage office window. Then the buck-toothed bastard reeled off the boardwalk and staggered into the street past the stage, holding his bleeding stomach. The stage team started kicking, whistling, showing white eyes, panicking.

Wolf rolled some more, dropped off the boardwalk and crammed against its edge, sighting up his Colt again over it. Kinder was on the boardwalk, pointing his gun in his direction. But it was clear to Wolf his sudden move sideways and drop to the boards had frustrated Kinder. Wolf aimed deliberately and fired as Kinder's Remington flamed.

Wolf became aware of a stab of pain in his shoulder, high up. But Kinder was staggering back, surprise on his lean face, his cold stare shocked.

Wolf triggered again. Kinder jolted as more lead hit him, but he raised his gun and fired once more. His lead ripped a groove across the boardwalk, exposing a blaze of white new wood. Missing Wolf, it ricocheted and exploded dust as it buried itself into the street near one of the stage wheels.

Then everything would have been silent except for Jaul's loud, awful moaning. Wolf saw the ex-Jayhawker was kneeling on the street, hunched over, holding his gut while drifts of steel-grey gunsmoke drifted leisurely past him up the street.

Kinder had slumped and was now sitting against the stage office tie rail. He was staring at Wolf. He was blinking and trying to raise his Remington again, still clasped in his hand. Wolf knew he wasn't going to make it. It was only Kinder's vicious urge to kill that was still motivating him. The man was trying to do his best to deny the Reaper's call, but he was fast losing the battle.

Then Kinder said, 'It's gittin' dark.' As he muttered it he went limp. This time Wolf knew Kinder's hard, vicious, unforgiving stare would never look upon another day. No more than ten seconds had elapsed from the first shot.

After moments, as the rush of blood caused by the gut-taut action subsided, Wolf became aware of a moistness in his shoulder. He looked down. He saw lead had scraped across the top of it, near his neck. It was seeping blood.

It was as he raised his eyes from the wound that he saw Bone Head coming out of the Lucky Dragon Eatery, napkin tucked up to his neck, knife and fork in his hand. He soon sized up the situation. When he'd taken it in he became wild-eyed. He began running down the street, throwing his knife and fork away and napkin as he did, his fat body wobbling, his rolling gait awkward, driven into unnatural action by his fear.

Wolf took off after him, soon came up on him. He jammed his gun into his back. Bone Head juddered to a halt. 'Fer Chris'sake sake, don't shoot, pardner.'

Wolf said, 'Turn around.'

Bone Head, hands elevated, swung 180°. His fatty eyes were round, fear-ridden when Wolf met them. 'What in the hell's goin' on, boy?'

Wolf's stare was hard, brittle. 'You pretendin' you don't know?'

Bone Head's jowls wobbled. A grain of potato was sticking to his chin. 'Would I be askin'?'

'You helped kill my Ma, Bone Head. What's a man supposed to do when faced with thet? Your dead leader jest tol' me you did.'

Gains's jaw dropped open. 'Kill your Ma? Hetch tol' yuh thet? Why the no good, God damned liar. I don't know nothin' about your Ma, boy, so help me God.'

Wolf's stare was steel hard. 'You don't? Let me take you back a leetle, Bone Head. November, '63? Beely Creek Valley? You were on a rampage through there. You fired a certain homestead. The woman came screamin' out of the buildin', ablaze. The man of the house was bein' dragged around the place before he was cut up. Then there was a kid on the trail, by the new bridge, when you was makin' your getaway run. Kinder gunned him down — '

Bone Head waved his brawny arms wildly, his eyes like a drowning man's clutching for the straw he hoped would save him. 'Hell, thet was way back. I wanted no part of it. It was awful. Thet's why I recall it. Jees, we weren't up to thet stuff most of the time. It was Kinder. He said he had scores to settle with the farmer. It was Layton an' Jaul who fired the house. I was out of it, shot up by the woman. Jaul put the first shot into her. I didn't do nothin'.'

'But you were there, Bone Head.'

Gains began to shake. He began screwing up his coat bottom in his fat hands. 'Aw, hell, it was the war, pardner. You know we all did things we shouldn't hev' in thet damned war.'

'Not all of us.' Wolf waved his gun. 'Where's Mitch Layton now? You know?'

Bone Head's eyes lit up. It was clear he was hoping to grasp the right straw this time — the one that would save him. 'Yeah. Yeah. Layton. It's Layton yuh want — him an' Jaul an' Kinder . . . they done the killin'.' Gains's stare pleaded pitifully with him this time. He gestured with a fat paw. 'I'll make a deal with you, pardner. If I give you Layton, do I go free? So help me, I didn't do no killin'.' He patted the leg Wolf had observed Bone Head favoured. 'I got this laig shot up. Your Ma. She did it. She was a real brave lady — firin' off thet damned shot-gun.'

Wolf cocked his Colt Army. 'Just give me Layton, then we'll see.'

Bone Head waved a quivering hand, pointing a finger towards God knew where. 'He's down on the Trinity, Texas, last I heard, gatherin' longhorns. He didn't want no part of us after Beely Valley. He quit the bunch, sick to the stomach he tol' me. He said he was quittin' the Jayhawkers, too. He took up with the regular war. Heard tell he fought at Spotsylvania . . . ' Bone Head's fat face crumpled. He began to shake. Tears began to trickle down his cheeks. 'Fer Pete's sake, Wolf, give me a break. I ain't done nothin' to yer kin. Jest fought a war, thet's all. I ain't a bad man.'

Wolf stared at this pathetic barrel of blubber. Maybe it *was* the war. War brutalized. Injured men's minds, their bodies. Men like Bone Head just got carried along by it, maybe thinking they were patriots. Many were just fodder for the cannons, pawns for the politicians and generals, believing all they had been told about duty, honour and justice and fighting for the Cause ... for God and Country. Wolf clamped his lips together. Well, after the blood and terror, some readjusted, he knew, others never did. That brought him to another thing. Where did he fit? When this trail of vengeance was over, would he be able to adjust, wash the blood off his hands, clear his head of all he had done?

Shattering his thoughts, he saw Bone Head was moving with fearsome swiftness, clawing for his Colt. He was making a strangled, whining, almost babyish noise. Wolf decided in that split second, Gains was clearly hoping, with his tears, he'd done enough to distract him long enough. The sonofa ...

Guns boomed. Bone Head was falling, his face a bloody mess from the blood pouring out from his right eye socket after Wolf's lead tore through it and into his brain. It was as the gunsmoke drifted away that Wolf became aware of blood trickling from a burn across his right cheek.

Then he realized his gun was being wrenched out of his hand and a hard voice was saying, 'I'll take that, mister. You got some explainin' to do.'

Wolf turned to see the town marshal, according to his hat band. He had his shot-gun levelled up. His deputy was beside him, also pointing a long-barrelled Greener . . .

12

Near the headwaters of the Trinity River, Texas, February 1867

'Sure, I'm sure,' Colm McDonnel reassured. 'Mitch Layton's gatherin' sixty miles south of Dallas. Near Benson's Crossin'.'

Wolf stared through the drizzling rain at the tall rider, seated astride his big roan. They were on the bluff overlooking the canyon they had ridden out of half an hour ago. Colm was one of a group of ten men, whose camp Wolf had rode into early last evening. They had a large gather holed up in a box canyon whose water from a seep at its head formed a creek that emptied into the Trinity. They had fenced off the canyon's entrance. Over supper, they'd talked about the Kansas Pacific Railroad pushing track across Kansas with the intention of establishing railheads for shipping cattle. A place called Abilene was mentioned and a man by the name of Joseph McCoy was offering to purchase all the beef the Texan ranchers could trail drive up there.

Wolf tipped his hat, to say goodbye. 'Waal, I'm obliged for your hospitality and your information, Colm. Hope you make the drive. *Adios.*' He swung the pinto and headed south, towing his pack mule.

It had been a long ride to here, through some bitter weather. The Denver police held him for nigh on two months, before they let him go. Three killings did take some explaining away, Wolf would be the first to admit that. It took Kelsy Jaul three days to die of his gut wound. He went into a coma soon after he was shot. He never recovered. The doctor said shock induced it and gangrene finished him off. The plea of self-defence Wolf offered, using the name of Johnson Bawdry, eventually carried the day, with the help of an enthusiastic Eastern journalist, out to capture the rip-roaring essence of the West. His defender claimed to have seen the whole thing. Wolf gave his name as Johnson Bawdry, because Wolf Strange was on the record as dead and he didn't want anything to hinder his determination to wreak revenge. Nevertheless, he abhored the need to use such deceit. Someday, maybe, he would be able to tell the real story . . .

* * *

After a week of hard, wet travelling he circled past Benson's Crossing, turned off a faint trail he had followed and camped by a small creek twenty miles to the south of the ford. He thought of stopping off at the crossing, but decided it was better not to advertise his presence in the vicinity. Benson was sure to remember him and the army post was only a few miles up the road. However, there was the possibility the trader wouldn't recognize him. For, when he hit Benson's Crossing the first time he'd been a hunted animal — leaned out, wild-eyed, a man on the run; a very different person to what he was now. Now he was relaxed, filled out after regular meals and long days in the saddle roping and riding and negotiating the long trail back to Texas. He was a little taller, too, older and . . . wiser? He reckoned some of Goodnight's counselling before they had parted hadn't been entirely wasted on him — about leaving the past where it was and focusing his whole attentions to the future. And now Kinder and the rest were out of the way he was even beginning to question whether or not to continue with the need to settle this last score. But then Ma's charred remains and Pa's mutilated body would haunt him, have him once more tossing, waking up sweating and crying out in the night. And he knew he would have to exorcise those horrific visions before he could know true peace. And the only way to do that, that he knew of, was to

261

eliminate the causes of his pain and nightmares.

He made camp back in the trees, in a bunch of rocks by a small creek and soon had a small fire going. For some time now — the whole day, in fact — there had been a gradual rising anticipation in him; a burning instinct insisting he was nearing the end of his search. Every fibre of his being was telling him it was so.

Happy to have a dry night camp for once, he turned the fatback sizzling in the pan, then poured himself coffee. It slid down his gullet, hot and welcome. But it was his Comanche pinto that destroyed his feelings of well-being by suddenly beginning to move restlessly, stare at the night and point its ears towards the trail they'd recently left. The crackling bacon forgotten Wolf tensed up, loosened the Colt in its holster.

Some moments later he heard the rumble of wheels, the crack of a branch being run over. Then he stood and stared at the fire-etched frame of the man driving a wagon. He was picking a trail for the wagon through the rocks to gain access to the camp. After more moments passed the driver finally steered the rig into the camp perimeter.

'Saw your fire,' the driver called.

Wolf said, 'You're welcome to supper.'

The loaded wagon negotiated, the driver climbed down and unhitched the horse from the shafts and picketed it near the pinto. As he came into the firelight Wolf saw he was a short, stocky man with a broken-toothed smile. 'Obliged,' he said as he hunkered down and warmed his hands by the fire. The night was cool, still and starlit. 'I'm Hank Sykes,' he added.

Wolf offered his hand. 'Johnson Bawdry.' He passed over his spare mug, filled it with steaming coffee. The man drank gratefully.

'Bin to the crossin',' Sykes said. 'Picked up some supplies. Saw your fire from the trail. Was figurin' on beddin' fer the night instead o' pressin' on, so I thought I'd make your acquaintance. We have a gather east of here. Boss intends to trail them to Kansas purty soon.'

Wolf lifted out the spitting bacon, laid it on his tin plate and cut some more off his slab of fatback and dropped it into the pan. He passed over the plate of bacon along with a hardtack biscuit. 'Ain't much,' he said.

'More'n welcome,' said Sykes affably. After chewing his first mouthful and swallowing it he went on, 'By your garb, you're into cows.'

'Rode with Goodnight an' Lovin'. Took a herd to Fort Sumner las' year.'

Sykes's stare had respect as it lifted to meet Wolf's gaze. 'I heard about thet. Heard they is gatherin' another herd. Thet right?'

Wolf tended to his bacon, hissing in the pan. 'Far as I know. Guess a lot o' other folk in Texas is doin' the same thing now, from what I've seen — those who hev' the guts to, thet is.'

Sykes wiped bacon fat off his chin with the back of a gnarled hand. He said, 'I'm with Mitch Layton. We got a sizeable herd penned up in a canyon east of here. He's lookin' fer hands. Took a herd to Sedalia las' year. Built himself a ranch on the proceeds, up there in the canyon. Brand he runs is the BL mark. You hear of it?'

Wolf had stiffened. *Mitch Layton?* Hit with the news, he kept his feelings hidden. 'No,' he said. 'He's lookin' fer hands, you say? Figure I'll ride in with you in thet case.'

Sykes beamed across the fire. 'Proud to have you along.' He helped himself to more coffee. From then on they talked about general things, long into the night. Trail loneliness could do that to men, Wolf had long since discovered.

They broke camp early. After three hours' ride they entered the canyon Sykes had talked about. A fence was strung across its mouth. A creek came out of it and headed towards the Trinity ten miles behind them. It was a lush strip of land, even this time of year. A fair-size herd of beeves grazed peacefully.

The closer Wolf got, the more tense he became. It was end of the trail. He was not happy about it, for the real purpose behind this ride was to kill once more. Making it worse, Sykes often spoke warmly of Layton. A man to ride for, he said, as they talked by the camp-fire. Even-handed in his handling of men, he extolled.

As they got further into the canyon a cold feeling scurried up Wolf's backbone. And it didn't help him to realize he was beginning to have feelings of regret about this.

'There's the ranch house,' said Sykes. He pointed to a large, low adobe dwelling on a rise of ground about a half-mile ahead. From there Wolf reckoned a man could see right down the canyon. A proud man would feel even prouder with such a mess of acreage stretching out before him and such a herd of cattle avaliable to sell at a Kansas Pacific railhead when he got them there.

They went past the corrals. Under the willow awning jutting out from the long frontage a man was standing, shading his eyes against the low sun. He had been watching their progress for some time. As they drew close, Wolf immediately recognized Mitch Layton, who had once been a frequent visitor at their farm when he had been a boy.

'Thet's the boss, on the stoop,' said Sykes. 'I'll leave you to it.' He veered the wagon off towards the back of the house.

Wolf went gut-taut, his heart thumping. At the tie rail before the house he reined up. He had seen hands riding out, heading for the mouth of the canyon. Mitch Layton looked as though he had been making ready to leave with them. A bay horse was tied to the rail, a double-girthed Texas saddle on its back. But he was stopped now, regarding him with steady eyes. Wolf saw his once dark hair was now completely grey. His lean face was teak coloured, severe, tight over his high cheekbones. His grey eyes were calm. It was clear he'd recognized him.

Layton said, 'I didn't believe the rumour you were dead. I figured you'd come by, some day.'

'You figured right,' Wolf said.

Layton tightened his lean lips for a moment, then said, 'Can't we talk?'

Wolf raised dark eyebrows. 'I don't think it would do any good.'

'No,' Layton said. 'Maybe not. I guess your ears are closed.'

Wolf edged his hand towards his Colt Army, but the click of a gun behind him being armed froze the move.

'I could tell him to shoot, Wolf,' Layton said, 'but I don't want to do thet. I'll tell you why. Since I quit the army I've worked hard here. I intend to work harder, build up somethin' real big. I don't want to lose it an' I've seen too much killin' in my life. It's time the killin' stopped.'

Though Layton was airing his own

feelings of late, Wolf said, 'You're wastin' your breath.'

Layton narrowed his eyelids, his gaze still direct, unafraid. 'I ain't proud of what happened to your folks. But thet was the way things went those days. You can't tell me you never did things you don't regret.'

Wolf was about to tell him he hadn't, but hesitated. There were things that happened, there were people who were killed when they could have been spared. Errol Blake killed a boy, no more than five years old. Unintentionally, but killed him. Errol had fretted about it for the rest of what life was left to him. Sometimes Wolf thought Errol had deliberately ridden into Captain Fenger's camp, knowing full well he wouldn't get amnesty and to get hanged to pay for it. In the heat of the skirmishes, the deadliness of them, there had been only moments in which life-and-death decisions had to be made. There was a woman once, she came running out from a house in one of the settlements they were raiding. Bullets were singing all around. He swung around, fired on reaction . . .

'I can't let it go,' he said.

'Esteban will shoot you,' Layton said. 'I have learned it is not in the nature of *vaquero* to stand by and see his *patrón* gunned down.'

'You could call him off,' said Wolf. 'We could settle this like men. You could tell him thet.'

'I could,' said Layton. 'I heard about the killin' of Jaul, Gains and Kinder in Denver. Figured it was you. I'll tell you, boy, Kinder was your man.'

Wolf said, 'You were all there at the farm.'

He climbed down from the pinto, deliberately wrapped rein around the tie rail. He was aware of the man behind him, but didn't turn around. He kept his eyes on Layton.

'I won't draw on you, Wolf,' said Layton. He lifted his gaze. 'Esteban. This is between men. Do not interfere.'

'But, *patrón* . . . '

'Do not interfere.'

'As you wish.'

Wolf drew swiftly, cocking his Colt as it came out of leather. Layton didn't move, left his hands by his side.

'Well, Wolf?' he said. 'Can you pull the trigger?'

Frustrated rage flashed through Wolf. He holstered the Colt. 'Now pull, damn you.'

He drew again. When Layton remained motionless he fired a shot. It hit an inch from Layton's boot, yet the ex-Jayhawker didn't flinch. Instead he said, 'I got to tell you your Pa killed a man before he died, Wolf. It tells me even the most passive of men get driven to extremes sometimes. But, that aside, d'you think your Pa would approve of this, wronged though he was?'

More rage flooded through Wolf. 'He's dead! It don't matter a damn now.' He stepped forward, put the gun against Layton's temple. A gasp came from Esteban. 'I could blow you to hell, Layton,' Wolf said.

He saw Layton's Adam's apple slide up and down his throat before he said, 'But you won't, will you?'

'Wolf!' It was a woman's voice that startled him, made him turn. He was stunned to see it was Jenny Braison standing in the ranch house doorway, her hand to her mouth her eyes round and startled.

Jenny came on until Wolf felt her hand grasp his arm. 'Don't do it. That's my cousin I told you about. He's a good man. I've explained to him about me and you. Damn it, you've got to know: *he saved your life, Wolf, down by the bridge thet day, at the risk of his own. Stopped Hetch Kinder from putting the killin' bullet into you.*' Jenny wrung her hands. 'You can't kill him. He's all I have, apart from you.'

'All you have . . . ' Wolf stared at her. 'Me?'

Jenny shook her head, clearly agitated. 'I said I'd follow you if you quit without me. But they held me at the post. Major Bryant, the commander, thought it best. Then the news of your death came.' Her eyes accused him. 'Thet hurt me, Wolf, you hear? Mitch tol' me what happened at the farm, when I explained about you an' why I left the dugout. Then we heard about the others bein' shot in Denver by a Johnson Bawdry. Mitch said it had to be you and someday you would come fer him.' Now her eyes turned tragic. 'Please, Wolf, don't kill him.'

Wolf lowered his Colt. It was all so stupid. Crazy. He couldn't find any words and was acutely aware Jenny was staring at him — Layton, too — as if waiting for the death sentence, or otherwise.

Mechanically, he holstered the Colt Army cap-and-ball, made a half turn. He stared at them for moments. Finally, he stammered, 'I gotta go. I can't stay.'

Jenny gave off a little gasp, grabbed his arm even harder, desperately it seemed. 'No! I won't let you go.' Her lips tightened. Suddenly the fire he had known came back into her eyes. 'I *will* follow you this time. To hell if I have to. But it'll hurt me bad to leave Mitch. He's been a father to me. Stay here, fer me.'

Layton said, his gaze level, 'I don't expect you to come to terms with things right off, boy. Maybe you never will. But me an' Jenny have talked about this. It jest depended on how you an' me came out of it when we did meet up.'

Wolf lifted his hands to the saddle horn. He found all sorts of emotions were tearing at him. Deep emptiness, sadness, frustrated vengeance, anger, remorse, all clawing at him, wanting a piece of him. Then, out of the bewildering maze, Goodnight's words when they had parted at Fort Sumner rang in his ears. 'It takes a real big man to forgive and forget a wrong done, Wolf. Think on that.'

'Wolf?' Jenny's voice cut across his confusion. Again he felt her hand rest on his arm. 'What are you thinking?'

Wolf felt his heart begin to pump.

Already the feelings he'd had for Jenny were renewing themselves, stronger this time. She had guts. And, knowing who he really was and what he had come to do, she could have rejected him. Family ties could be powerful. Layton could have had him shot down like a dog, soon as he had ridden up, but he didn't. He had been prepared to risk his own life to prove his sincere regret and wish for reconciliation, if only for Jenny's sake.

On an impulse, Wolf let his hands drop off the saddle horn. He lifted the right one. He touched Jenny's raven hair. As before, during that hair-raising ride from the dugout to Benson's Crossing, the contact thrilled him and Jenny pressed to meet it. He said, 'It'll take time, I guess. But, gittin' the drift, we got plenty of thet, I reckon.' He extended his hand towards Layton. Layton took it warmly.

Soon, there'd be a herd to take to Abilene. Real men were needed to drive it.

*Other titles in the
Linford Western Library:*

THE CHISELLER

Tex Larrigan

Soon the paddle-steamer would be on its long journey down the Missouri River to St Louis. Now, all Saul Rhymer had to do was to play the last master-stroke of the evening. He looked at the mounting pile of gold and dollar bills and again at the cards in his hand. Then, looking around the table, he produced the deed to the goldmine in Montana. 'Let's play poker!' But little did he know how that journey back to St Louis would change his life so drastically.

THE ARIZONA KID

Andrew McBride

When former hired gun Calvin Taylor took the job of sheriff of Oxford County, New Mexico, it was for one reason only — to catch, or kill, the notorious Arizona Kid, and pick up the fifteen hundred dollars reward the governor had secretly offered. Taylor found himself on the trail of the infamous gang known as the Regulators, hunting down a man who'd once been his friend. The pursuit became, in every sense, a journey of death.

BULLETS IN BUZZARDS CREEK

Bret Rey

The discovery of a dead saloon girl is only the beginning of Sheriff Jeff Gilpin's problems. Fortunately, his old friend 'Doc' Holliday arrives in Buzzards Creek just as Gilpin is faced by an outlaw gang. In a dramatic shoot-out the sheriff kills their leader and Holliday's reputation scares the hell out of the others. But it isn't long before the outlaws return, when they know Holliday is not around, and Gilpin is alone against six men . . .

THE YANKEE HANGMAN

Cole Rickard

Dan Tate was given a virtually impossible task: to save the murderer Jack Williams from the condemned cell. Williams, scum that he was, held a secret that was dear to the Confederate cause. But if saving Williams would test all Dan's ingenuity, then his further mission called for immense courage and daring. His life was truly on the line and if he didn't succeed, Horace Honeywell, the Yankee Hangman would have the last word!

MISSOURI PALACE

S. J. Rodgers

When ex-lawman Jim Williams accepts the post of security officer on the *Missouri Palace* river-boat, he finds himself embroiled in a power struggle between Captain J. D. Harris and Jake Farrell, the murderous boss of Willow Flats, who will stop at nothing to add the giant sidepaddler to his fleet. Williams knows that with no one to back him up in a straight fight with Farrell's hired killers, he must hit them first and hit them hard to get out alive.

THE CONRAD POSSE

Frank Scarman

The Conrad Posse, the famous group that had set about cleaning up a territory infested by human predators, was disbanding. The names of the infamous pistolmen hunted down by the Posse were now mostly a roll-call of the dead, but the name of the much sought Frank Jago was not among them. That proved to be a fatal mistake for it was not long before Jago took to his old trail of robbery and murder. Violence bred violence, and soon death stalked the land.